The Firebird in Russian folklore is a fiery, illuminated bird; magical, iconic, coveted. Its feathers continue to glow when removed, and a single feather, it is said, can light up a room. Some who claim to have seen the Firebird say it even has glowing eyes. The Firebird is often the object of a quest. In one famous tale, the Firebird needs to be captured to prevent it from stealing the king's golden apples, a fruit bestowing youth and strength on those who partake of the fruit. But in other stories, the Firebird has another mission: it is always flying over the earth providing hope to any who may need it. In modern times and in the West, the Firebird has become part of world culture. In Igor Stravinsky's ballet *The Firebird*, it is a creature half-woman and half-bird, and the ballerina's role is considered by many to be the most demanding in the history of ballet.

The Overlook Press in the U.S. and Gerald Duckworth in the UK, in adopting the Firebird as the logo for its expanding Ardis publishing program, consider that this magical, glowing creature—in legend, come to Russia from a faraway land—will play a role in bringing Russia and its literature closer to readers everywhere.

ALSO BY GAITO GAZDANOV

The Spectre of Alexander Wolf
Night Roads
Buddha's Return

AN
EVENING
WITH
CLAIRE

A NOVEL

GAITO GAZDANOV

Translated from the Russian and with
an Introduction by Jodi Daynard

OVERLOOK DUCKWORTH / ARDIS
NEW YORK • LONDON

This edition first published in paperback in the United States
and the United Kingdom in 2014 by
Overlook Duckworth / Ardis Publishers, Peter Mayer Publishers, Inc.

NEW YORK:
141 Wooster Street
New York, NY 10012
www.overlookpress.com
For bulk and special sales, please contact sales@overlookny.com,
or write us at the address above.

LONDON:
Gerald Duckworth & Co. Ltd.
30 Calvin Street
London E1 6NW
info@duckworth-publishers.co.uk
www.ducknet.co.uk
For bulk and special sales, please contact sales@duckworth-publishers.co.uk,
or write us at the above address.

Library of Congress Cataloging-in-Publication Data

Gaito Gazdanov.
[Vecher u Kler. English]
An evening with Claire / Gaito Gazdanov;
translated & with an introduction by Jodi Daynard.
p. cm.
ISBN 0-88233-934-6
I. Title.
PG3476.G39V413 1988   891.73'44—dc 19   87-34492 CIP

Book design and typeformatting by Bernard Schleifer
Manufactured in the United States of America
ISBN: 978-1-4683-0884-6 US
ISBN: 978-7156-4917-6 UK

2 4 6 8 10 9 7 5 3 1

Go to www.ardisbooks.com to read or download the latest Ardis catalog

Acknowledgments

The translator would like to thank Marina Brodskaya, who first introduced me to Gazdanov's work and whose painstaking comparison of the English text against the Russian made this a much better translation than it would otherwise have been. Thanks also to Mark Polizzotti for his insightful editorial suggestions, and to Rita and Victor Tupitsyn for reading the translation. Needless to say, I take full responsibility for any inaccuracies that crept by their exacting eyes.

Introduction

Nobody could have foreseen, that January 1930 in Paris when *An Evening with Claire* was published, just how enormously successful it was going to be. At the age of twenty-six, Gaito Gazdanov had published a handful of stories in Marc Slonim's Prague publication, *Volya Rossii* (The Will of Russia), and received guardedly positive reviews from such harsh critics of the emigration as Georgi Adamovich and novelist Marc Aldanov. But he was still an unknown, a very young man from whom no one expected an overnight bestseller. Within a month of publication the verdict was in: "Gazdanov's *An Evening with Claire* is a true artistic event in young Russian emigré literature," wrote Mikhail Osorgin in the first review of *Claire*.[1] Marc Slonim commented, "All of the emigré critics have justly noted *Claire* to be one of the brightest literary phenomena of recent times." Even the generally hard-to-please Adamovich had to admit that the novel was "very talented, in some places very fine . . ."

But the instant popularity of *An Evening with Claire* reached far beyond its critics. The novel, it seems, touched a nerve within Europe's emigré population as a whole. In Berlin, a reviewer's effusive praise captures this general enthusiasm: "You don't paint with sharp, passionate colors. Your tone is gentle and tender. Your tone is not exotic: it is quite simple and very Russian . . . Your book . . . has allowed us to feel the waves of the secret movements of life, allowed us to feel what you yourself felt when, as a child, you heard the stories your father told you about the Indian Ocean."[2]

Part of *Claire*'s appeal, surely, was that it presented prerevolutionary Russia and the cataclysmic events which destroyed it in a manner both real and wistful, unregretful yet tender. Neither sentimental nor callously forgetful, it described a past the emigré community of its time could, without shame, call their own. But for M. Gorlin, and undoubtedly for many other readers, Gazdanov's first novel offered more than just a taste of Old Russia. It offered, too, an awakening of hope, a ray of optimism about the future. After all, what was the initial experience of emigration itself if not that of a ship sailing on a vast, treacherous yet thrilling ocean? Half a century later, *An Evening with Claire* still strikes us with its lyricism, its psychological depth and vivid depiction of an extinct way of life.

Luckily for the student of émigré literature, Gaito Gazdanov was not a man who looked far beyond his own experience for creative material. From all accounts (notably Laszlo Diene's monograph, Russian *Literature in Exile: The Life and Work of Gaito Gazdanov*), *An Evening with Claire* presents a fairly accurate picture of the author's life up to the age of twenty. Georgi Ivanovich Gazdanov was born on December 6 (New Style), 1903, in St. Petersburg, into an upper middle class Russian Orthodox family of Ossetian origin. His mother, Maria Nikolaevich Abasieva, came from a monied aristocratic family; she was a cultured woman with an enormous passion for literature. His father, Ivan Sergeevich Gazdanov, gained a degree in forestry when the boy was three, at which time the family left St. Petersburg to spend the next six years on the move—to Siberia, Minsk, Smolensk, and, later, to the Ukraine, where Gaito was to attend school. Gaito's father died when the boy was only eight but, as *Claire* plainly shows, he retained vivid memories of his father's life and death. Gaito also had two sisters, both of whom died at a young age.

In 1912 Gaito was enrolled in a military school in Poltava; the reasons for this are unclear, but it may be gleaned from descriptions in the novel that after the death of her husband and one of the daughters, Gaito's mother became too despondent to care adequately for her son. Gaito hated the rigid military etiquette of his new school; unable to adjust, he soon became known as an "arrogant" and "rebellious" troublemaker. *Claire* recounts the time a religion teacher pompously (and rhetorically) declared that any student who felt God was no longer a viable subject for study could leave the class. To everyone's surprise, Gazdanov stood up and left the room.

The year 1919 should have been Gazdanov's year of graduation from the gymnasium in Kharkov. But the Civil War was at its peak and the young man, caught up in the general excitement, chose instead to join the army. For the next two years he traveled southern Russia on the machine gun platform of an armored train. It is clear from the novel that Gazdanov's decision was not motivated in the slightest by political conviction: "I wanted to know what war was," he states. It was a part of "that same desire I always had for the new and unknown. I joined the White army because I was on her territory, because it was expected of me; if the Reds had occupied Kislovodsk at that time, I most certainly would have joined the Red army."

While for others the harsh years of the Civil War would be forgotten as quickly as possible, for the young author they provided a wealth of material—enough for nearly a decade of fiction. The war—described in the latter half of Claire—afforded him the kind of experience and insight into human character that few generally experience in a lifetime. Hangings, famine, the treachery and bravery of soldiers and officers—although still a boy, Gazdanov was able to test his own strength, define the limits of his own personality. In his second novel, *Istoriya odnogo puteshestvie* (The History of a Journey), Gazdanov admits that "the revolution was the best thing he ever knew."

Although the author's attitude toward the events of 1914–19 was to modify with time and the sad experience of emigration, it became a mark of his character to measure the value of experience subjectively, seeking to find its meaning, not to judge it.

With the defeat of General Vrangel's army in November 1920, Gazdanov was forced to evacuate the Crimea along with thousands of others. He landed in Gallipoli, on the southwestern shore of Russia. Of this experience the author writes, "We knew that we were leaving; but we understood this only objectively, and our imaginations didn't reach further than the sea and the boat: a new and unusual echo reached us, as if issuing from those countries to which we had not yet been but which now we were fated to discover." A year passed before Gazdanov was able to reach Constantinople. Here, in 1922, he resumed school and graduated from the Sumen Gymnasium in Bulgaria in September 1923.

That winter, Gaito arrived in Paris. He was twenty years old. His husky build and the physical rigors of soldiering were to pay off. For the first six years of emigré life he was forced to accept various unskilled labor jobs; he heaved sacks to and from the barges at St. Denis, washed locomotives, and worked as a driller in a suburban Citroen factory. Apparently, Gazdanov had few friends in Paris or, if he did, refused to impose on them: In the winter of 1925–26, he slept on benches and in subways, forced to beg for enough money to eat. In spite of these enormous hardships, though, the author must have been writing steadily.

Marc Slonim remembers the day—it was in the beginning of January 1927—he received a mysterious package from one "completely unfamiliar" Gaito Gazdanov. The package contained the author's first story to be published in emigration, "Povesti o trex neudachnikov" (Stories of Three Failures). Slonim read the story and was immediately impressed: "The episodes about the Civil War were rendered in an original, amusing, and lyrical manner; portraits of living people stood out clearly, and throughout the story one had the sense that a brilliant, fully developed storyteller was at work." But the editor could find no return address on the package. His co-workers at the paper were certain that the strange name "Gazdanov" was a pseudonym for an established emigré author. But Slonim stood his ground, convinced that he had found a young, new talent. Predictably, one month after the story's publication he received a joyous letter from its twenty-four-year-old author. From then on, Gazdanov's stories were to appear regularly in the pages of *Volya Rossii*.

Even before his first story was published, Gazdanov had begun to frequent the Parisian emigré literary groups. The first of these was the "Young Writers Club," which in the spring of 1925 became the "Union of Poets and Writers." It was a large group that held many literary soirees in which Gazdanov actively participated. It is likely that he met a number of the older generation's writers here, including Boris Zaitsev and Victor Balmont. He may also have met some of the "Montparnassians," among them the poet Boris Poplavsky, whom Gazdanov greatly admired. The Montparnassians were members of the new "bohemian" literary generation who flocked to cafés along Boulevard Montparnasse to exchange ideas. Even though Gazdanov certainly had contact with them, he was a loner by nature, fiercely independent, and slow to align himself with any group. In 1926-27 Gazdanov attended the meetings of Georgi Adamovich's *Zveno* and, after his "discovery," began attending Slonim's own gathering, *Kochev'e*. It is here that Gazdanov would read many of his own stories and, eventually, recite passages from *An Evening with Claire*.

Spring of 1928 was an important time for another reason as well. After six years the author hit upon a workable "second career": night taxi driving. Under the circumstances it was a brilliant choice. Since he often made enough money on weekends alone to sustain him the following week, cab driving allowed Gazdanov ample time to write. It was a job he would retain for the next twenty-three years.

The new métier brought with it a modicum of physical comfort and free time. What it could not do, however, was bring an end to the emotional alienation the author shared with many of his peers. As late as 1934 Gazdanov would write, "We live, neither Russians nor foreigners, in an airless expanse without means, without readers, without anything at all ... in this fragile Europe, with the incessant feeling that tomorrow everything will go to the devil, as it did in 1914 and 1917. All that is left us is to manipulate fictional heroes if we don't want to revert to a past which we never knew, or such exclusively emigré themes which make you sick with all your soul."[3] *Claire* captures the sensibility of those who, "neither Russians nor foreigners," were seduced by Europe but could never truly call her their own.

A year after the appearance of *An Evening with Claire*, Marc Slonim wrote, "The awful experience of the last decade has cast doubt upon everything, created an enormous rift not only in our experience, but in our psychology, in our approach to art, in our understanding of literature. And a writer cannot fail to feel the heightened pressure which the reader places on him. Moreover, the reader is right: He wants literature to be for him what it was for whole generations of Russian intelligentsia: something that counts, that has depth, that raises the same burning questions of individual and social life—this is the fundamental direction the 'true tradition of Russian literature continuing its tradition abroad."[4] It is interesting to note that while Gazdanov strongly resisted the idea of himself as a "traditional" Russian writer, he falls squarely within his mentor's definition of one. As A. Novik, another critic of the period, recognized, Gazdanov was deeply concerned with "the most difficult and eternal questions of life."[5] Indeed, this quality may have been part of his allure to the older critic and to others seeking—however unconsciously— to find the torch of Russian literature ablaze in Europe, to salvage their culture from the wreckage of war and exile.

But the critics of *An Evening with Claire* failed, by and large, to notice the torch Gazdanov was carrying. They hastened instead to attribute his work to more immediate influences, such as Marcel Proust and Ivan Bunin. Gazdanov's connection to Proust, established in Osorgin's first review of the book, was echoed by all subsequent reviewers. It is a link that has been especially hard to break.[6]

It is true that, like the beginning of Proust's novel, *Claire* opens with a man who cannot sleep and who goes on to record the thoughts and memories that occur to him in the course of the evening. And, like Proust, Gazdanov's narrative method is based on streams of internal associations. Yet, in an interview conducted shortly before his death in 1971, Gazdanov stated that he hadn't read a word by the French author until World War II. His admiration had been instantaneous, and later in life he considered Proust "the greatest writer of the twentieth century."

There are other places, however, from which Gazdanov could have derived his model for *Claire*. In his lectures on Proust, Vladimir Nabokov himself points out that the French author "had a precursor." The precursor was Leo Tolstoy. Nabokov illustrates his argument with a scene from *War and Peace*, but this reader can rake an even earlier example, from the writer's first (unfinished) work, *A History of Yesterday*: "I am writing a history of yesterday, not because yesterday was extraordinary in any way, for it might rather be called ordinary, but because I have long wished to trace the intimate side of life through an entire day. God only knows how many diverse and diverting impressions, together with the thoughts awakened by them, occur in a single day." It is entirely possible—though we will never know for certain—that the young Gazdanov came to Proust's side accidently, by way of his own compatriot.

Ivan Bun in, the second of Gazdanov's "models," was a writer who made his reputation before the revolution. In his review of *Claire*, Adamovich states that the novel contained "something of Proust, something of (Bunin's) *Zhizn' Arseneva* (The Life of Arsenev)." Adamovich reiterates his conviction in a 1934 article in which he called Gazdanov "Bunin's only true disciple."[7] Bunin himself greatly respected the younger writer's "stylistic mastery," and some uncanny similarities do exist between the two novels. But while the young author was certain to have had access to some of Bunin's works, those most cited in connection to *Claire*—especially *The Life of Arsenev*, which was published the same year—were almost certainly out of his reach. From hindsight it seems that Bunin's ties to Gazdanov—as in the case of Proust—were only coincidental.

But so much for debunking specious theories. Contemporary readers of *Claire* will quickly discover that, for better or worse, Gazdanov had his own very definite ideas about art. "It seems to me," he wrote in an early article on Edgar Allan Poe, "that art becomes real when it manages to communicate the stream of emotional fluctuations which make up the history of human life and the richness which defines the scope of every individual. The realm of logical deduction, children's mental games, the blind directedness of reasoning, the ultimate codifying of accepted rules—these disappear as soon as the force of another psychic order—or disorder—begins to act. Each of our judgments is reduced to a concession to the senses."[8]

Gazdanov's idea of the importance of the senses quickly grew to include the idea of the necessary search—via these senses—for meaning. This idea is fully articulated in "The Third Life," a story published in 1932. But the extraordinary sensuality of *Claire* and, importantly, the conclusions which the hero derives from his sensual experiences, point to the fact that these ideas were active much earlier; *Claire* was perhaps Gazdanov's first extended journey in search of the meaning of life.

The author's philosophical convictions worked against him with the critics. They lamented his lack of imagination, his autobiographical heroes and his books' general lack of plot. In an article that appeared in 1930, Vladimir Weidlé praises the inventiveness of Vladimir Sirin (a pseudonym for Nabokov) and cites Gazdanov's utter lack thereof.[9] Elsewhere, Adamovich repeatedly criticizes Gazdanov for "having nothing to say but saying it brilliantly." But Weidle and the other critics missed the point: The peculiar quality of Gazdanov's fiction derives precisely from the fact that his primary concern was not to fictionalize life, but to understand it. Unlike Vladimir Nabokov, with whom the young author was often compared, Gazdanov did not place art above everything else. For him, art was not a "necessary illusion," the "unreal estate" so cherished by the former, but a vehicle through which ideas and, ultimately, meaning could be attained.

There is an interesting consistency in the fact that while Gazdanov lamented the emigration and the state of postwar Europe in general, Nabokov felt only indifference toward it. In his 1936 article on young emigré literature, Gazdanov wrote, "The awful events which the young litererary generation were witness to or participants of destroyed all 'Weltanschauungen,' 'world-views,' 'world-feelings,' dealt them a fatal blow. And everything that this generation had previously believed to be certain and indisputable was swept away forever."[10] Several years earlier, by contrast, Nabokov had said, "In these days, when a gray Soviet anniversary is being celebrated, we are celebrating ten years of contempt, fidelity, and freedom. Let us not curse exile. Let us repeat today the words of the ancient warrior about whom Plutarch wrote, 'During the night, desolate fields far from Rome,

I would pitch my tent, and my tent was Rome to me.'"[11]

Interestingly, it was Gazdanov who first noticed Nabokov's seeming immunity to the cataclysmic events surrounding him. Gazdanov concludes his discussion above by adopting Tolstoy's view that a writer must have a "proper moral relation" to his subject and that, for emigré writers, such had become impossible. In other words, argues Gazdanov, the artist—even one whose primary concerns are internal or psychological—cannot work in a cultural and social void. There was only one exception: Vladimir Sirin. "But he is an exception only by the strength of the specialness, the remarkably rare kind of gift he possesses—he is a writer existing outside of society, of nationality, of the rest of the world . . . Sirin has no relation to young emigré literature."[12]

Gazdanov possessed a very different kind of talent. As Laszlo Dienes has said, he was always trying "to harmonize the world," to reconcile his own joyous sense of wonderment with the depressing material and moral conditions of his times. Marc Slonim's obituary of the author confirms this impression: "I quickly realized that his biting sarcasm, his harsh judgements about people, books and politics, and his airs of the arch-cynic were masks or, rather, defense mechanisms for a very sensitive, even sentimental dreamer seeking truths and beliefs, and with difficulty accepting the awful world."[13] That Gazdanov could not allow himself the luxury of art for art's sake comes as no surprise. As his work demonstrates, he was not interested in creating new worlds but in discovering a meaning or "proper moral relation" to this one. A master stylist, for Gazdanov the language of fiction was never an end in itself but a means of expressing the emotions and fullest contours of the human soul. *An Evening with Claire* marked the beginning of this quest, the first complete articulation of the man as artist.

The success of *An Evening with Claire* opened many doors for the young man. It gained him entry into the prestigious journals, allowed him to publish his thoughts freely with a readymade audience. By the onset of the Second World War, Gazdanov had published an array of new stories, a second novel, and parts of two new novels (one of which, *The Flight*, was abandoned; the other, *Night Roads*, was published in completed form in 1952). He also met his wife-to-be, Faina Dmitrievna Gavrisev. During the war the author devoted much of his time and energy to staying financially afloat and to resistance activities, specifically with a group of Soviet refugee partisans (see *Je m'engage a defendre Paris: Defense de la France*, 1946). After the war, Gazdanov was offered a job at Radio Liberty in Munich, which he enthusiastically accepted, eventually becoming their chief bureau editor. From this post, which he was to keep until his death, the author broadcast (under the pseudonym of Georgi Cherkasov) literally dozens of literary essays on topics ranging from Dostoevsky to Sartre.

Although Gazdanov went on to attain literary distinction for a number of other works, nothing he did ever quite achieved the purity, the beauty, or the simple charm of *An Evening with Claire*.

Jodi Daynard

1. *Poslednie Novosti*, February 6, 1930.
2. "Pokhval'noe Slovo Gaito Gazdanovy," Rul', March 1930.
3. "Literaturniya priznaniya," Vstrechi 6.
4. *Novaya Gazeta*, March 1931.
5. *Volya Rossii* 3/4, 1931.
6. As recently as 1982, Temira Pachmuss describes Gazdanov (in *A Russian Cultural Revival*, Tennessee University Press) as "another writer of the Proustian school."
7. Pollednie Novosti, 16 February 1934.
8. *Volya Rossii* Sj6, 1929.
9. "Otvet na anketu ob emigrantskoi literatury," *Chisla 2/3*.
10. *Sovremennie Zapiski* 60.
11. Rul', November 18, 1927.
12. Ibid.
13. *Novae Russkoe Slovo*, December 19, 1971.

A Note on the Translation

The prose of Gaito Gazdanov is deceptively easy to translate. He is not one of those authors who revelled in the kind of word-play, double-entendres or puns which may be found in abundance in Russian literature of this period. However, *Claire* did present two specific difficulties which may benefit from elucidation. The first was the author's unusual use of the past imperfect tense, normally used for repeated actions but here almost completely replacing the past perfect. In the opening section of the book where the hero reminisces about his growing relationship with *Claire*, this gives the impression that each event is suspended in time, infinitely repeated, infinitely nostalgic. An overly zealous or literal use of the author's device could easily have been confusing. I have tried to retain something of the original's extraordinary wistfulness while preserving its narrative clarity.

The other difficulty in translating *Claire* is—for want of a better word—its introspection. Much of this novel is an attempt to describe an internal landscape, one fluid with emotions, moods, and perceptions. Lacking a psychological language the author, in order to be precise, resorted to long, often convoluted phrases. Sometimes, in this attempt at emotional precision, the author loses the gossamer lyricism of his narration; sentences become overly stiff and formal. Much of what Gazdanov sought to describe would have been greatly aided by the new—if distastefully literal—language of Freud, but in the second decade of the century such was hardly common parlance: It certainly was nor accessible to a young emigré like Gazdanov. I have thus resisted the temptation to substitute his verbal wrestlings with the more streamlined terminology of modern psychology.

—J.D.

AN
EVENING
WITH
CLAIRE

*C*LAIRE HAD BEEN ILL; I HAD BEEN SPENDING EVERY EVENING with her and, after taking my leave, would invariably miss the last metro and end up going on foot from rue Raynouard to Place St. Michel, which was not far from where I lived. I would walk past the Ecole Militaire; from there one could hear the clanging of the chains to which the horses were tethered and smell the dense equine odor so unusual for Paris; I would then stroll down the long, narrow rue Babylone and at the end of this street, in the artificial light of distant street lamps, the face of an illustrious writer, composed of sloping planes, would stare at me from the window of a photographer's studio; a pair of omniscient eyes behind European horn-rimmed glasses followed me halfway down the block until I finally crossed the black, glittering strip of the Boulevard Raspail. At last I would reach my hotel. Resolute old ladies in shabby dress hobbled past me on their weak legs; above the Seine, drowned in darkness, shone a myriad of lights, and when I stared at them from the bridge it would begin to seem as if I were standing above a harbor and that the sea was covered with foreign ships on which lanterns had been set ablaze. After glancing back at the Seine a final time I would go up to my room, lie down, and instantly sink into the profound gloom; strange forms stirred within this gloom which sometimes had no time to form into familiar images before my eyes and would vanish, having never materialized; and in my sleep I would regret their disappearance, sympathize with their imaginary and incomprehensible sorrows, and I lived and dozed in this ineffable state which I could never recapture while awake. This should have distressed me but in the morning I would completely forget about what I had seen in my sleep, and the last memory of the previous day would be that I had once again missed the train. In the evening I'd set off again for Claire's. Her husband had left for Ceylon several months earlier: We were alone, and only the maid, bringing tea and biscuits on a wooden tray with a frail chinaman delicately drawn on it, a woman of about forty-five who wore a pince-nez and for this reason was unlike a servant, always brooding about something and forgetting either the sugar tongs or the sugar bowl, a saucer or spoon—only this maid disturbed our little twosome as she entered the room and asked whether Madame needed anything else. And Claire, who for some reason was certain that the maid would take offense if you did not ask her for anything would say, "Yes, please bring us the grammophone from Monsieur's study," although nobody wanted a grammophone and after the maid had left it would remain exactly where she had put it down and Claire would instantly forget all about it. The maid came and went four or five times in an evening, and when I mentioned to Claire that her maid was certainly well preserved for her age and that her legs possessed a positively youthful indefatigability, but that all the same I thought she was not quite right in the head—either she had a movement mania or simply an undetected but unquestionable weakening of the mental capacities related to the onset of old age—Claire looked at me pityingly and answered that I would do better to exercise my special Russian wit on others.

And first of all, according to Claire, I should have remembered that yesterday I once again appeared in a shirt with two different cufflinks and that I could not, as I had done the day before yesterday, simply throw my gloves down on her bed and grab Claire by the shoulders, something that wouldn't pass for a proper greeting anywhere on earth, and that if she wanted to enumerate all my violations of the elementary rules of propriety she would have to talk for . . . here she thought for a moment and said: five years. She said this with a serious face and I began to feel sorry that such trivialities could upset her and I wanted to ask her forgiveness. But she had turned away and her back began to tremble; she brought her handkerchief to her eyes and when, finally, she looked at me, I saw that she was laughing. She told me that the maid was just recovering from her latest love affair, and that the man who had promised to marry her now refused in no uncertain terms. "That's why she is so pensive." "What's there to brood about in that?" I asked. "So he refused to marry her. Does it really require so much time to comprehend something so elementary?" "You always put the question too simply," said Claire. "With women that just can't be done. She's pensive because she's upset, can't you see?" "Did the romance last a long time?" "No," Claire answered. "Two weeks in all." "That's strange. She's always been like that," I remarked. "A month ago she was just as melancholy and distracted as she is now." "My goodness," said Claire, "she was simply having another love affair then." "So it is actually quite simple," I said. "Forgive me, I didn't realize that behind the pince-nez of your maid lay concealed the tragedy of a female Don Juan who, however, wants someone to marry her, contrary to the Don Juan of literary renown who disapproves of marriage . . ." But Claire interrupted me, reciting with great pathos a phrase which she picked up from a billboard and which, upon reading, made her laugh until tears came to her eyes:

> Happy owners of the true 'Salamanders'
> Never abandoned by the builder!

Then the conversation returned to the topic of Don Juan, passing somehow to ascetics, then to the arch-priest Avvakum, but coming to the temptation of St. Anthony I halted, since I remembered that Claire didn't much care for that sort of talk. She preferred other subjects, such as music or theater; but most of all she loved jokes, of which she knew many. She would recount these extraordinarily witty and thoroughly indecent jokes, and then the conversation would take a strange turn and the most innocent phrases would seem to conceal double entendres, and Claire's eyes would begin to shine; yet when she had stopped laughing her eyes grew dark and criminal and her thin brows knit. But as soon as I moved closer to her she would say in an angry whisper, "But you're mad!" and I would step back. She smiled and her smile clearly said, "My god, is he naïve." Then, continuing the interrupted conversation, I began to inveigh against things towards which I normally felt completely indifferent. I tried to sound as harsh and offensive as possible, as if to take vengeance for the defeat I had just suffered. Claire mockingly agreed with all my arguments and because she conceded so easily my own defeat became even more apparent. "Yes, mon petit, that's very interesting," she would say, not concealing her laughter which referred, however, not to my words but to my defeat, and by emphasizing this scornful "lá" she demonstrated that she didn't attach the slightest meaning to any of my arguments. I pulled myself together, once again resisting the temptation to draw nearer to Claire as I understood that it was already late, and forced myself to think about something else. Her voice reached me half-muffled; she was laughing and telling me all kinds of nonsense which I listened to with strained attention until I noticed that Claire was simply entertaining herself. It amused her that at such moments I could not understand a word she said. The next day I came to make amends. I promised myself not to approach her and to choose only those topics which would eliminate any danger of repeating the previous evening's humiliating moments. I spoke of all the sorrows I had known, and Claire recounted, in her turn, the death of her mother.

"Sit here," she said, pointing to the bed. And I sat down right beside her and she rested her head on my knees and said, "Yes, mon petit, it's sad, we are unhappy even so." I listened to her, afraid to move, as if my slightest movement would offend her sorrow. Claire slowly stroked her hand from side to side across the blanket, and it was as if her sorrow were exhausted in these movements which, at first unconscious, began to attract her attention and ended with her noticing the poorly trimmed cuticle of her little finger and reaching out to the scissors on the night table. Once again she smiled a lingering smile, as if she had perceived and traced within herself some long train of memories which had ended on an unexpected, though not unhappy, thought; and Claire glanced at me with instantly darkening eyes.

Gingerly I placed her head on the pillow and said, "Excuse me, Claire, I've forgotten my cigarettes in the pocket of my raincoat," and went out to the foyer; I could hear her soft laughter coming from the other room. When I returned she remarked, "I was surprised just now, I thought you always carried your cigarettes with you, in the pocket of your trousers, as you have done up until now. Have you changed your custom?" She looked me in the eye, laughing and pitying me, and I knew that she knew perfectly well why I got up and left the room. To top it all off I was careless enough even then to take a cigarette case out from the back pocket of my trousers. "Tell me," said Claire as if entreating me to tell her the truth, "what's the difference between a raincoat and a pair of trousers?"

"Claire, that's very cruel," I answered.

"I don't recognize you, mon petit. Put the record-player on again, it'll distract you."

That evening after I said goodbye to Claire I overheard the cracked and faint voice of the maid coming from the kitchen. She was mournfully singing a cheerful song and it surprised me:

> It is a pink blouse
> With a small woman inside,
> Fresh as a newly blossomed flower,
> Simple as a wildflower.

She put so much melancholy into these words, so much vain sorrow, that they began to sound different from usual and the phrase "fraiche comme la fleur éclose" immediately reminded me of the maid's elderly face, her pince-nez, her love affair and her eternal pensiveness. I told Claire about this and she felt sorry for the unhappy maid, because nothing of the sort could happen to Claire and because this sympathy did not arouse her own emotions or apprehension—and she was also quite fond of the song:

> It is a pink blouse
> With a small woman inside.

She would give this verse the most diverse inflections—at times questioning or assertive or festive and mocking. Every time I heard this tune on the street or in a café I would start to feel out of sorts. Once I went to see Claire and began to curse the song, insisting that it was too French, that it was cheap and that no self-respecting composer would be taken in by such a piece of frivolity; this was precisely the main difference between the French way of thinking and serious things. I said, "This art is as unlike the real thing as fake pearls are to genuine ones. It lacks the main ingredient," I went on, having already exhausted my arguments and growing angry with myself. Claire nodded her head, then took my hand and said:

"There's only one thing missing."

"Namely?" She began to laugh and sang:

> It is a pink blouse
> With a small woman inside.

When Claire had recovered and had already been out of bed for several days, either in the armchair or the chaise lounge, and felt completely well, she asked me if I would accompany her to the motion pictures. Afterwards we sat for nearly an hour in a café. Claire was quite short with me, interrupting me often; when I made a joke she would restrain her laughter and, smiling in spite of herself, say "No, that's not funny." And because she was, it seemed to me, in such a bad mood, she projected her own dissatisfaction and irritability onto everyone else. In astonishment she asked me: "What is wrong with you tonight, you're not yourself," although I wasn't behaving out of the ordinary. I escorted her home; it was raining. When I kissed her hand at the door she said irritably, "Well, come on in and have a cup of tea." She said this in such an angry tone that one would have thought she wanted to drive me away: "Well, get out of here! Can't you see I'm sick of you?" I entered. We drank our tea in silence. I felt uneasy and, going up to her, said: "Claire, don't be angry with me. I have waited to be with you like this for ten years. I ask nothing of you." I wanted to add that such a long wait entitled me to request at least the simplest, most minute concessions, but Claire's eyes had turned from grey almost to black; I noticed with horror—for I had waited far too long and had long ago ceased hoping for this moment—that Claire had come right up to me and that her breast was pressing against my buttoned, double-breasted coat. She embraced me, her face drawing nearer to mine. The chilling smell of the ice cream she had eaten at the cafe suddenly struck me unusually and Claire said, "How could you not have understood?" as a tremor swept through her body. Claire's cloudy eyes, gifted with the power of so many metamorphoses—cruel one moment, shameless or laughing the next—I saw these turbid eyes in front of me for a long time, and when she had fallen asleep, I turned my face towards the wall and a former sorrow visited me. This sorrow was in the air and its transparent waves floated above Claire's white body, along her legs and breast; sorrow escaped from Claire's mouth in invisible breath. I lay next to Claire and could not fall asleep. Glancing away from her pale face I noticed that the blue of the wallpaper in Claire's room suddenly seemed lighter and strangely transformed. The dark blue which I saw in front of my closed eyes always reminded me of a mystery that had been solved; and this resolution had been dark and sudden, as if it had frozen before having succeeded in revealing everything completely. It was as if the effort of some kind of spirit had stopped in its tracks and died, and in its place this dark blue background had sprung up. Now, as if the effort had not yet come to an end, it had turned light, and in becoming lighter the blue had discovered within itself this dull-mournful shade, so oddly in keeping with my feelings and undoubtedly related to Claire. Light-blue apparitions with lopped-off hands sat in the room's two armchairs; they were indifferently hostile to one another, like people whom the same fate has befallen sharing the same punishment but for different crimes. The lilac border of the wallpaper curved in a wavy line like the conditional designation of the path by which a fish swims in the deep-blue sea; through the fluttering curtains of the open window a distant current of air was striving to reach me but failed. It, too, was tinted in the same light blue and brought with it a long gallery of memories, which fell as regularly and as irrepressibly as rain. But Claire turned, waking up and muttering, "You're not asleep? Go to sleep, dear, you'll be tired in the morning," and once again her eyes seemed to cloud over; she didn't have the strength to overcome her torpid slumber and, scarcely having uttered the phrase, fell back asleep. Her brows remained raised and in her sleep she looked as if she were surprised at what was happening to her. There was something extraordinarily characteristic in this surprise: Surrendering to the power of sleep, or sadness, or yet another emotion, no matter how strong the emotion was she never ceased being herself; and it seemed that the mightiest tremors were powerless to alter this perfectly completed body, could never destroy this final invincible charm which had induced me to waste ten years of my life in pursuit of Claire, and which had made it impossible for me to get her out of my mind at any time, any place. "But in every love there is sorrow," I remembered. Sorrow for the end and approaching death of love, if it has been a happy one, and, if the love has been in vain, sorrow for that which never belonged to us. And how I longed for the riches I did not possess, as earlier I had grieved that Claire belonged to another; and how too now did I grieve, lying on her bed in Paris, in the light blue clouds of her room which until this evening I would have thought unattainable, indeed non-existent, the clouds which circled above the white body of Claire covered in three places by such shameful and agonizingly alluring hair, that never again could I dream about Claire as I had always dreamed about her, and that much time would have to pass before I would come to form another image of her and before this image would become in its own way just as unattainable for me as had been this moment, this body, this hair, these light-blue clouds.

I thought about Claire, about the evenings I had spent with her, and gradually I came to remember everything that went before them; and the impossibility of understanding and expressing all of it weighed heavily upon me. This evening it was even more apparent than usual that there was no way for me to embrace and feel that endless succession of ideas, impressions and sensations which, in their totality, rose up in my memory like a row of shadows reflected in the dim and fluid mirror of a seasoned imagination. It was to music that I owed the most wonderful, the most intense emotions that I had ever felt; but I am only able to strive perpetually for music's enchanting and momentary existence—I cannot live it. Quite often at a concert I would suddenly begin to understand things which had eluded me up until then; the music would suddenly awaken strange physical sensations which I had thought myself incapable of feeling. But with the last dying notes of the orchestra these sensations would vanish and once again I would find myself in the obscurity and uncertainty that was so often a part of me. The illness which had created in me the improbable state between the real and the imaginary consisted in my inability to distinguish the various efforts of my imagination from the genuine, spontaneous feelings which events aroused in me. It was like the absence of the gift of a spiritual sense. In my eyes every object was almost entirely devoid of precise physical boundaries, and because of the severity of this strange deficiency, I was never able to do even the most feeble drawing; later, in school, try as I might I could not picture the complicated lines of a sketch, although I understood the obvious result of their combination. On the other hand, my visual memory had always been well developed and to this day I don't know how to reconcile this blatant contradiction. Such was the first of those innumerable contradictions which later were to plunge me into impotent reverie; they reinforced my awareness of the fact that I could not penetrate to the core of abstract ideas, and this awareness in turn engendered uncertainty in myself. I was thus quite timid, and the reputation I had in childhood for being an insolent boy could be explained, as several people (for example, my mother) saw it, by my strong desire to overcome this perpetual lack of self-confidence. Later on I developed the habit of associating with the most diverse people and I even developed certain rules of conversation which I very rarely transgressed. These consisted in the use of several dozen subjects which, accessible to any interlocutor, seemed complex but were actually quite primitive; but I found the essence of these simple, conventional and obligatory rules thoroughly alien and devoid of interest. I was nonetheless unable to master my own petty curiosity, and it gave me the greatest pleasure to induce people to talk about their innermost selves; their humiliating and worthless confessions never fully aroused what might have been my rightful and understandable disgust. It should have, but it never did. Perhaps this was because it was unusual for me to have strong negative feelings about anything: I was far too indifferent to external events; my deaf inner existence remained incomparably more significant to me. In childhood this inner existence was, in any case, more connected with the outer world than later on; gradually it left me, and in order to return to that dark place with its heavy, palpable air, I had to cover a distance which became greater as my life experience—that is, my supply of visual or sensory experience—became greater.

From time to time, horrified, I would think that perhaps the day would come when I would no longer be able to return to myself, and that I would turn into an animal. At this thought a canine head, hungrily devouring leftovers from a heap of garbage, would appear in my memory. But that perilous intimacy between the imaginary and the real, which I considered my illness to be, was never far off; every so often, during attacks of mental fever, I would be unable to feel my own existence; I could hear a ringing in my ears and suddenly on the street I would have such difficulty walking that it was as if I were struggling to push forward with my heavy body into that dense air, those dark landscapes of my fantasies where the startled shadow of my head glided so effortlessly. At such moments my memory abandoned me.

My memory was always the most flawed of my faculties, although I could easily memorize whole printed pages. Memory covered my recollections with translucent glassy webs and destroyed their lovely clarity; the memory of feelings was immeasurably richer and more powerful than the memory of thoughts. I was never able to go back as far as my first sensation; I didn't know what it had been. I became conscious of my surroundings and first understood its causes when I was about six; eight years from the time of my birth, thanks to the rather large quantity of books which they locked away from me but which I managed to read anyway, I was capable of expressing my thoughts in writing. At that time I wrote a long story about a hunter of tigers. I could recall only one occurrence from my early childhood: I was three years old; my parents had returned to Petersburg, which they had left not long before. They were planning to stay only a short time, about two weeks. They stayed with my grandmother in the big house where I was born on Kabinetsky street. The windows of the fourth floor apartment looked out onto a courtyard. I remember that I was left alone in the living room and was feeding my toy rabbit a carrot which I had procured from the cook. Suddenly, strange sounds issuing from the courtyard caught my attention. It sounded like a quiet purring interrupted from time to time by a prolonged, metallic ringing that was very delicate and clear. I went up to the window, but as it didn't occur to me to stand on tiptoe, I didn't manage to see anything. Then I slid a large armchair over to the window, clamored up on it, and from there climbed onto the windowsill. Even now I can see before me the deserted courtyard below and the two woodcutters; they were moving back and forth like badly made mechanical toys. Every once in a while they stopped to rest, at which point the sound of a suddenly-halted and vibrating saw would ring out. I stared at them as if transfixed, and unconsciously began crawling out of the window. All the extremities of my body were dangling into the courtyard. The woodcutters caught sight of me; they halted what they were doing, raised their heads and stared up, but without uttering a word. It was the end of September; I remember that suddenly I felt a cold draft and my hands, not covered by my sleeves, began to freeze. Just then my mother walked into the room. Quietly she approached the window, snatched me up, shut the window-and fainted dead away. I remember this event vividly; I can recall still one other occurrence which took place considerably later, and both of these memories instantly transport me back to my childhood, to that period of time which I am no longer able to understand.

The second event was the following: Shortly after I had learned to read and write, I read a story in a small children's primer about a village orphan whose teacher, out of kindness, took him into the school. He helped the warden heat the oven: cleaned the classroom and studied diligently. But the school burned down and the boy spent the winter out on the streets in the blustery cold. No book since has made such an impression on me: I could see the orphan before my eyes; I pictured his dead mother and father and the burned-out ruins of the school; and my grief was so strong that I cried for two days in a row, ate practically nothing and barely slept. My father finally lost his temper and said, "See what happens! You taught the boy to read so early and look what comes of it! He should be running about, not reading. Thank God there's still time—and why on earth do they put stories like that in children's books anyway?"

My father died when I was eight. I remember how Mother brought me to see him in the clinic. I hadn't seen him in the month and a half since he first became sick and I was struck by how emaciated his face had become, by his black beard and burning eyes. He stroked my head and, turning to Mother, whispered:

"Take care of the children."

Mother was unable to answer him. Then he added with unusual force:

"My God, if only they would tell me that I'll be a simple shepherd, just a shepherd, but that I will live."

Then Mother led me out of the room. I went into the garden: Sand crackled under my feet; it was hot and bright outside, and one could see far into the distance. Sitting in the carriage with Mama I said:

"Mama, Papa didn't look so bad. I thought he would look worse than that." She didn't reply, but only pressed my head to her knees and like that we rode home.

There was always something ineffably sweet about my recollections. It was as if I no longer saw or knew anything that happened to me beyond the moment I chose to resurrect: I would find myself first a cadet, then a schoolboy, then a soldier, and that was all; everything else would cease to exist. I grew accustomed to living within a past reality which my imagination had brought back to life. Once inside, I had unlimited power. I obeyed no one, no solitary will; for long hours as I lay in the garden I would create fictitious situations for all the people in my life, and I would make them do just what I wanted, and this continual pastime of my fantasy gradually grew into a habit. Right after this came a period in my life when I lost myself and could no longer even recognize myself in self-portraits. I read a lot during this time; I remember the portrait of Dostoevsky on the first volume of his works. They took this book away from me and hid it, but I broke the glass door to the bookcase and, out of all the books inside, pulled out the very one with the portrait. I read everything indiscriminately, but I didn't like the books they gave me to read and couldn't bear the "Golden Library" collection, with the exception of the tales of Andersen and Hauff. At that time my individual existence was nearly imperceptible to me. While reading *Don Quixote* I would imagine everything that happened to him, but the work of my imagination carried on without me, and I myself made almost no effort. I couldn't participate in the heroic deeds of the Knight of the Sorrowful Countenance, nor would I laugh at him or Sancho Panza; it was always as if I were not there and Cervantes' book was being read by someone else. This period of intense reading and development, this former era of my completely unconscious existence might, I believe, be compared to a most profound mental swoon. I had only one feeling left, a feeling which grew to full maturity at that time and afterwards never left me: that of a transparent and distant sorrow, groundless and pure. Once, having run away from home and walking along a grey-brown field, I noticed a frozen layer of snow in a distant ravine that was glistening in the spring sun. Its white and delicate light rose up suddenly in front of me, and I found it so rare and lovely that I nearly wept with emotion. I set off for this place and reached it after a few minutes. Crumbly and dirty snow covered the black earth; it weakly glimmered a bluish-green, like a soap bubble, and was nothing like that sparkling snow which I had seen from far away. For a long time I was to remember the naive and sad feeling that I had experienced at that moment, and the snow drift, and several years later, while reading a moving book that had no title page, I imagined the spring field and the distant snow and the few steps it took before I saw the dirty, melting dregs. "And is there nothing else?" I was to ask myself, and life seemed just like that: I would live out my life on earth a certain number of years, come to my last minutes, and then die. "What? And nothing more?" These were the only movements of my soul at the time. Meanwhile, I read foreign writers, filled myself with the contents of strange lands and eras, and this world gradually became my own; I saw no difference between Spanish and Russian settings.

I came out of this state after a year, nor long before I entered the gymnasium, and by then my feelings were all familiar to me; henceforth it was only my external accomplishments, all quite meaningless and unimportant, which grew. My inner life began to exist in spite of immediate events, and all the changes which came about within it did so in the dark, independent of my notes for conduct, school, punishment or failure. Those times of complete withdrawal into myself came less frequently and with less force, and only rarely did they return to me like attacks of a fading but incurable illness.

My father's family often moved from place to place, nor infrequently covering huge distances. I remember the bustle, the packing of cumbersome items, and the eternal questions about just what was in the basket with the silver, and what was in the basket with the fur coats. Father was always cheerful and amiable while Mother maintained a severe demeanor; it was she who handled all the cares of packing and traveling. She would look at her small gold watch that in those days hung around her neck, and was always afraid of being late. And Father would calm her down by saying with an expression of surprise on his face, "We've still got plenty of time."

He, on the other hand, was always late for everything. Three days before he was to leave he would think of it and say, "Well, this time I'll be on time," and invariably after all the kisses, farewells, and my little sisters' tears, he would return home after half an hour.

"I simply don't understand how it could have happened. I

had at least fourteen minutes to spare! Then I arrive at the station and they tell me the train has just pulled out. It's unbelievable."

He was always busy with chemistry experiments, geographical work, and public affairs. These absorbed him so completely that often he would forget about everything else, as if nothing else existed. But there were two other things which interested him, namely, fires and hunting. When there was a fire he displayed unusual energy. He would retrieve whatever he could from a burning house and, as he was quite strong, often saved whole cupboards—which he carried out on his back—from the flames. Once, in Siberia, when the house of one of the rich merchants was burning, he managed to rescue a safe by means of a wooden ladder. As it turns out, not long before the fire he had appealed to this same merchant with a request that the merchant rent out one of the apartments in his house; but the latter, having found out that Father was not a merchant, had refused in no uncertain terms. After the fire he came to us and asked Father to move into that house, and he even brought us presents. Father had forgotten about the fire: He was glad to help anyone who needed it, but was not drawn simply by sympathy for people whom misfortune had befallen; he also nourished an incomprehensible love for fire. The merchant, meanwhile, insisted. "How could I have known that you would rescue my safe?" he asked simple-heartedly. Father finally remembered what had happened, became angry and sent the merchant packing with the words, "This is all a lot of nonsense you're talking and I'm busy."

He liked physical exercise, was a good gymnast and an indefatigable equestrian. He always laughed at the "seat" of his two brothers, dragoon officers who, he said, had not learned to ride "even by the time they'd finished the equine academy and besides, even in childhood they had no talent for riding and went to the equine academy only because you didn't have to take algebra there." He was also a wonderful swimmer. In places where the water was deep he would do an unusual thing, something I never saw anywhere else: He would sit as if on land and not in water, carry his legs so that his body formed a sharp angle, and suddenly begin to spin like a top: I remember how I sat naked on the shore, laughing; and then, arms clinging to Father's neck, I would swim across the river on his broad, hairy back. Hunting was his passion. Sometimes he would return home in a *rosvalni* after twenty-four hours of painstaking and exhausting hunting, and from the sleigh the glassy, dead eyes of an elk stared out; he hunted for auroch in the Caucasus, and thought nothing of going several hundred miles for a simple invitation to go hunting. He was never sick, didn't know the meaning of fatigue, and would sit in his study, which was filled with flasks, retorts and cases with some kind of viscous substance in them, for hours on end, then later leave for three days of wolf hunting and little sleep, and when he returned would sit back down behind his desk as if nothing had happened. His perseverance was extraordinary. He spent an entire year modeling a relief map out of plaster, a map of the Caucasus, in the most minute geographical detail. It was already finished. For some reason I went into Father's study; he wasn't there. The map was standing on the bookshelf. I extended my hand towards it, pulled it toward me—it fell to the ground and shattered to bits. On hearing the noise Father came in, looked at me reproachfully and said, "Kolya, don't ever go into the study without my permission."

Then he sat me on his shoulder and went to see Mother. He told her that I had broken the map, adding, "Imagine, the map has to be done all over again from the beginning." He set to work and by the end of the second year the map was finished.

I didn't know my father very well, but I knew what was most important about him: He loved music and would listen to it for long periods of time without moving or getting up from his place. On the other hand, he hated the sound of a bell. Everything that reminded him in any way of death remained hostile and incomprehensible to him; this explained his aversion to cemeteries and monuments. Once, I saw Father extremely agitated and disturbed, something which almost never happened. This was in Minsk, when he learned about the death of one of his hunting buddies, a poor clerk; I didn't know his name. I remember that he was a tall man with a bald spot and colorless eyes who dressed badly. He always grew unusually animated when he spoke about partridges, hares or quails; he preferred small game. "Wolf, that's not hunting, Sergei Alexandrovich," he would say angrily to Father. "That's kid stuff. Wolf and bear are kid stuff."

"What do you mean, 'kid stuff'?" Father said indignantly. "And elk? And wild boar? Do you even know what a wild boar *is*?"

"I don't know what a wild boar is, Sergei Alexandrovich, but I repeat, you can't change my mind."

"Well, God be with you," Father said, unexpectedly growing calm. "But is tea also kid stuff?"

"No, Sergei Alexandrovich."

"Well then, let's go drink some tea. You're always busying yourself with birds. Now I'll see how much tea you can drink."

Our frequent visitors in Minsk included this clerk and the artist Sipovsky. Sipovsky was a tall old man with angry brows, a *borziatnik* and art lover. He was massive and broad-shouldered; his pockets were conspicuously deep. Once, coming to visit us and finding no one at home besides myself and the nanny, he looked at me with a steady gaze and then said abruptly, "Have you ever seen a rooster?"

"I have."

"And you're not frightened?"

"No."

"Here, look." He reached into his pocket and took out a huge, live rooster. The rooster began to clack its claws on the floor and spin around on its forelegs.

"Why do you have a rooster?"

"I'm going to draw it."

"He's not going to sit still."

"Then I'll make him sit still."

"No, don't force him."

"No, I won't force him."

We went into the nursery. Nanny, waving her hands, drove the rooster there. Sipovsky held him with one hand and with the other he drew a chalk circle on the floor; to my amazement the rooster lurched forward once or twice and then stopped and stood still. Sipovsky quickly drew it. I remember another drawing—a hunter, bending to the side, is leaping onto a horse. Directly in front of him two Borzois are chasing a wolf. The hunter's face is red and distressed; all four legs of the steed seem intertwined. Sipovsky gave me this painting as a present. I loved nearly all pictures of animals and knew a great number of breeds and wild beasts without having ever seen them, and had read three volumes of Brehm twice from beginning to end. Once during this time, when I was reading the second volume of *The Life of Animals*, Father's bitch, an English setter, gave birth to pups. Father distributed the blind puppies to acquaintances and kept only one pup, the strongest, for himself. Three days later, in the evening, the clerk came to us.

"Sergei Alexandrovich," he said without even greeting us, tears in his voice, "have you given away all the pups? What? Did you forget about me?"

"I forgot," Father answered, looking awkwardly at the floor.

"There's not one left?"

"There's one, but that's mine."

"Give it to me, Sergei Alexandrovich."

"I can't."

"I, Sergei Alexandrovich," said the clerk despairingly, "am an honest man. But if you don't give me the pup I'll have to steal it."

"Go ahead and try."

"And if I steal it and you don't notice?"

"Then you're in luck."

"Will you demand it back?"

"No."

When he left Father laughed and said with satisfaction, "Now that's a hunter. That's something I understand." He was extremely content and when the pup actually did disappear after a few days, he grew angry for appearances' sake and even said, "Well, what do you know, you can't keep anything at home." Nanny unexpectedly agreed with him, saying, "Today a dog, tomorrow it'll be our samovar." My sister, unusually curious, asked Mother: "And then it will be the piano, right, Mama?"

But apparently nobody really mourned the dog's disappearance in the least. The clerk didn't show up for two weeks, and then he appeared. "How's the dog?" asked Father. The former only grinned and said nothing. This puppy grew up very quickly. He was called Treasure; quite often when the clerk came to see us Treasure would come running behind him, and we thought of the dog as nearly a part of him. One time—it was a bright autumn day, Father had gone somewhere and Mother was reading by herself—Treasure darted out from a corner with his tongue thrust out and his muzzle covered with blood. He rushed up to me, began to squeal, grabbed me by the breeches with his teeth, and rugged me out of the house. We went through the Jewish quarter on the outskirts of town, went beyond the city, then into a field, and there I saw the clerk lying motionless on the grass, face down. I prodded him, called out, peered into his face, but he remained motionless. Treasure licked his face where blood was drying, trickling onto his mutilated bald spot. Then the dog sat on his hind legs and began to howl; he started to choke from wailing and then yelped, then once again began wailing. I was awestruck. There were the three of us in the field, a breeze was blowing from the river; the horrible old gun lay near the clerk's head. I don't remember how I got home. As soon as I saw Father I told him everything. He ran out without saying a word and galloped away on a horse which they had not even had time to unsaddle yet, as he had just arrived. He returned after twenty minutes and explained that the clerk, while clumsily recharging his gun, had blown his brains out loading a powerful shot. Father was very upset for several days, didn't joke, laugh, or even caress me. During lunch or dinner he would suddenly stop eating and become lost in thought.

"What are you thinking about?" Mother would ask.

"What a senseless thing," he would say. "What a stupid way to go. He is no longer, and there's nothing to be done about it."

And only after some time had passed did he become his old self again and, as before, tell each evening the continuation of the endless story about how the whole family was traveling on a ship of which I was captain.

"We're not taking Mama with us, Kolya," he would say. "She's afraid of the sea and would only disturb the brave voyagers."

"Let Mama stay home," I agreed.

"So then, we are sailing together to the Indian Ocean. Suddenly a storm gathers. You're the captain and everyone turns to you and asks you what to do. You calmly give your orders. What are they, Kolya?"

"Lower the lifeboats'" I cried.

"Well, it's still early to lower the lifeboats. You say, 'set the sails and fear nothing!'"

"And they set the sails," I continued.

"Yes, Kolya, they set the sails."

In the course of my childhood I completed several trips around the world, discovered a new island, became its ruler, built a railroad across the sea, and brought Mama directly to my island in a wagon, because Mama was so afraid of the sea and was not even ashamed of the fact. I became accustomed to hearing the story of the voyage in a boat every evening, and grew so used to it that when occasionally it would stop—for example, if Father had to go away—I was so upset I nearly cried. But then later, sitting on his knees and gazing from time to time into Mother's tranquil face, as she was usually by his side, I would experience true happiness, the kind that is accessible only to a child or to a person who possesses unusual spiritual strength. And then the story ended forever—my father became ill and died. While he was dying he said, as he gasped for breath:

"Only please, I beg you, bury me without priests, and without church rites."

But he was buried by a clergyman nonetheless. The bell he so disliked pealed, and in the quiet graveyard tall weeds grew rampant. I kissed the waxen forehead; they had brought me over to the coffin and Uncle held me up, as I was too little to reach. That moment when, clumsily dangling from Uncle's hands, I peered into the coffin and saw the black beard, the moustache and closed eyes of my father, was the most horrible moment of my life. The tall vaults of the church hummed, Aunt's dresses rustled, and suddenly I saw the inhuman, stony face of my mother. At that very second I suddenly understood everything; an icy feeling of death enveloped me, and I became aware of a sick frenzy, having all at once seen my own end somewhere in the infinite distance, the same fate as that of my father. I would have been happy to die at that very instant in order to share my father's fate and to be together with him. Everything darkened before my eyes and they brought me over to Mother; her cold hand rested on my head. I looked at her but Mother didn't see me, nor did she know that I was standing beside her. We went directly home from the cemetery: The carriage bobbed up and down on its springs, my father's grave was left behind . . . the air shook in front of me. Farther and farther silently glided the horses backs; we return home, but Father lies there motionless; with him perished my lovely ship and I, and the island with the white buildings I discovered in the Indian Ocean. The air wavered in my eyes; a yellow light suddenly flashed unbearably sunny flames in front of me, the blood flowed to my head and I felt very sick. When we got home they put me in bed; I had diphtheria.

The Indian Ocean and the yellow sky above the sea and the black boat slowly cleaving the water. I am standing on a footbridge, pink birds fly above the stern, and the burning hot air gently rings. I am sailing in my pirate vessel, but I'm sailing alone. "Where is Father?" And just then the boat comes across a wooded embankment; through a telescope I see Mother's strong ambler flash through the branches, and behind it at a long bold trot comes Father's black steed. We hoist the sail and for a long time we sail on, level with the horses. Suddenly Father turns to me. "Papa, where are you going?" I cry, and his toneless, far-off voice answers something unintelligible. "Where?" I repeat. "Captain," says the navigator, "the man is being taken to the cemetery." And, sure enough, the empty hearse was moving slowly along the golden road and the white coffin shone in the sun. "Papa has died!" I cry. Mother bends over me. Her hair is loose, her dry face is frightening and stony.

"No, Kolya, Papa hasn't died."

"Set the sails and fear nothing!" I command.

"A storm is coming!"

"He's screaming again," says Nanny.

But then we are crossing the Indian Ocean and we drop anchor. Everything sinks into darkness: The sailors are asleep, the white city on the bank is asleep, my father sleeps in the deep blackness somewhere not far from me, and then across our sleeping boat the black sail of the Flying Dutchman wildly billows.

After some time I got better and Nanny sat for hours by my bedside and told me all kinds of stories, and I learned many interesting things from her. She told me that on the streets in Siberia they sell frozen circles of milk, that at night people leave provisions on windowsills for the fugitive convicts who wander the fierce winter through towns and villages. For my parents life in Siberia, according to Nanny, was wonderful.

"The mistress didn't know the first thing about housekeeping," said Nanny. "Nothing. She couldn't tell the difference between chickens and ducks. There were lots of chickens but none of them laid eggs. They bought eggs in the market. The eggs were cheap, thirty-five kopeks for a hundred, not like what it costs here. A pound of meat cost two kopeks. And they sold butter in kegs. But the housekeeper was very sly. Once the master was calmly walking down the street when an old lady came up to him.

"'Do you know by any chance where the chief forester lives?' Us, that is. He said, 'I know. And who is it you wish to see?' 'Their housekeeper,' she says. 'She,' she says, 'is selling eggs very cheap—it's more expensive at the market.' They went shopping together, the old lady in front and behind her, the master. Well, the housekeeper confessed everything and cried, how she cried! It was shameful."

"Nanny, what about Vasilievna?"

"Now I'll tell you about Vasilievna. The mistress hired a cook, she was already a stern woman, about fifty, or maybe thirty."

"How can that be, Nanny, that's a big difference."

"It's not a big difference," said Nanny vehemently. "Listen or I won't tell you the story."

"I won't interrupt again."

"Her name was Vasilievna. She says, 'I am not from these parts, but I have a son in penal servitude. I myself am from Petersburg. I can cook anything,' she says, and it was true she could cook anything. Life went on, then one day the mistress had asked guests over. Vasilievna was making a pie and they set the table during the day. In the evening the mistress comes home, on horseback as she always did, a good horse, a bay, although bays are ill-suited for us but still good. So she comes in and sees nothing, nor a thing! There's no pie, the dishes are scattered everywhere. She goes into the kitchen and there's Vasilievna sitting all red in the face and in an absolute rage, so help me God. The mistress asked, 'Why isn't everything ready? What's the matter, Vasilievna?' And Vasilievna answers, 'I'm a lady myself, so don't yell at me like that! I don't want to serve anymore, I want to eat too.' And sure enough, the pie had been bitten into in several places. Then Vasilievna ran out of the house and didn't return for six days. She came back dirty, shabby, her clothes in rags and herself in tears. 'Forgive me,' she says, 'when I'm on such a drinking binge there's nothing to be done.' She's a big perfectionist."

"Who is, Nanny?"

"A perfectionist? Vasilievna. And now go to sleep; your illness will go to sleep too and afterwards it will pass. Sleep."

It was an airy, gossamer day when I went out for the first time. Small white clouds were scurrying away; but already in the east a cold air was turning blue, and I thought it must have been on just such a day that Andersen's field mouse, sheltering Thumbelina, bolted the door of his home, inspected the supplies of grain, and in the evening as she was going to sleep, said: "Well, now all that remains is to have a wedding. You must thank the Lord, for not all grooms have a fur coat like a mole, and please don't forget that you're a dowerless girl."

I felt sorry for Thumbelina and especially sympathized with the fact that she was lonely, because I had spent my whole childhood alone. However, I did not shy away from my peers; I played war and hide-and-seek and was, in the opinion of many,

even too sociable. But I never loved anyone and would leave
those from whom circumstances would separate me with no re-
grets. I got used to people quickly and, once accustomed, would
cease to notice their existence. This was, perhaps, a love of solitude, but in a rather strange, complex form. When I found myself alone I would always want to listen to something; others
prevented me from doing so. I didn't like to indulge in confi-
dences, but as my imagination was accustomed to acting quickly,
cordial talk came easily to me. Although I didn't lie, neither did
I express what I thought. Involuntarily I repelled the burden of
candid declarations, and I had no friends. Later on I understood
that in acting this way I had erred. I paid dearly for this mistake,
forfeiting one of the most valuable opportunities: I understood
the words comrade and friend only in a theoretical sense. I made
an unbelievable effort to create the feeling within myself, but I
succeeded only in understanding and feeling the friendship of
others. Then suddenly I grasped it to the core. It became especially precious when the spectre of death or old age appeared,
when much of what was acquired together now was lost together. I thought: Friendship means we're still alive and others
have died. I remember while I was studying in the military school
I had a friend named Dikov; we became friends because both of
us knew how to walk on our hands. Later we were no longer to
see each other, as I was taken out of the military school. I remembered Dikov only along with everyone else and never
thought solely about him. One hot day many years later, in Sevastopol, I saw a wooden cross in a cemetery and a nameplate
with the inscription: "Here lies the Timofeev cadet Dikov, who
died of typhus." At that moment I felt that I had lost a friend.
God knows why this strange man had become so close to me, as
though I had spent my entire life with him. I noticed then that
the feeling of loss and sorrow is especially strong on beautiful
days, when the air is particularly light and fresh; it seemed to me
that the same states were in my soul and that somewhere far
within me quiet was growing, replacing that soft, incessant noise
of my spiritual life which I almost never hear but which always
plays, and which weakens only slightly at some moments. This

means that a catastrophe has taken place. And I would imagine a huge expanse of land flat as a desert and visible to the very end. The remote edge of this space suddenly becomes severed by a deep crack and falls silently away, dragging with it everything on it. There is quiet. Then soundlessly a second layer breaks off and then a third, until all that remains is a few steps before the edge; finally, my legs sink into the crumbling sand. I fly with difficulty in the slow-moving, sandy clouds, down toward where everyone else has already fallen. There, just above my head, a yellow light burns and the sun, like a colossal lantern, lights up the black water of a still lake and the orange dead earth. I felt wretched and, as always, thought about Mother, whom I knew less well than Father and who always remained enigmatic to me. She didn't resemble Father in the least, either in her habits, her tastes or her character. It seemed to me that concealed within her was the danger of internal explosions and the continual conflict of selves which was entirely overt in myself. She was a very tranquil woman, somewhat cold in demeanor, who never raised her voice. Petersburg (where she had lived until her marriage), Grandmother's sedate house, governesses, scoldings, and the mandatory readings of classical authors had all exerted their influence upon her. The household servants, never afraid of Father even when he would cry in his resounding voice, "The Devil knows what this is!" always feared Mother, who spoke slowly and never lost her temper. From my very earliest childhood I remember her unhurried movements, the coldness which emanated from her and her courteous smile. She almost never laughed. Rarely did she caress children. If I ran to greet Father and leapt onto his chest (knowing that this strong man only occasionally pretended to be a grown-up but essentially was just like me, my peer) and if I were then to ask him to come into the garden and drive the toy carriage with me he would think about it for a moment—and then go. Mother, on the other hand, I approached slowly and decorously, like a well-brought-up boy should, and like someone who most certainly would not allow himself to shout with delight or rush headlong into the living room. I was not afraid of Mother: In our home they never punished us, nei-

ther myself nor my sisters; but I couldn't stop feeling her superiority over me—an inexplicable but undeniable superiority and
one that in no way depended upon her knowledge or abilities,
although actually these were exceptional. Her memory was altogether infallible; she remembered everything she had ever
heard or read. She spoke French and German with an irre-
proachable exactness and correctness, something which may perhaps have sounded too classical; but in Russian as well my
mother—for all her unaffected manners and her dislike of pretentious expressions—used only literary terms and spoke with
her usual coldness and indifferent-disdainful intonations. She
was always this way; only for Father would she suddenly smile
an irrepressibly happy smile from across the table or in the living
room, something which I would never see elsewhere under any
circumstances. She often scolded me—calmly, pronouncing
everything in a very steady voice. Meanwhile Father would look
at me with sympathy in his eyes and nod his head, as if lending
me his mute support. Then he would say:

"Well, God be with him, he won't do it again. You won't,
will you, Kolya?"

"No, I won't."

"Well, go on then."

I would turn to go and he would remark in an apologetic
tone, "In the end it'd be a shame if he were a little sissy and not
a naughty boy. Still waters run deep."

While giving me reprovals and explanations as to why it was
necessary to act in such a way and not another, Mother almost
never spoke with me; that is, she did not recognize the fact that
I could object. Once I remember I tried to answer back to her;
she looked at me with surprise and curiosity, as if just then noticing that I possessed the gift of speech. But I was the least gifted
member of my family: My sisters, on the whole, took after my
mother in the quickness of their understanding and their phe-
nomenal memory, and they developed more quickly than I did;
they never made me feel this way but I knew it quite well myself.
In childhood just as later on, I was alien to envy; I loved my
mother very much despite her coldness. This gentle woman was

like the incarnation of a painting and, as if guarding within herself this wonderful stillness she was, at the same time, not at all what she appeared to be. It took me years to understand this; and once I had, I sat for many hours imagining her real, as opposed to her apparent, life. She loved literature with such a passion that it became strange. She read often and copiously; when she finished a book she wouldn't speak or answer my questions; she would look directly in front of her with unmoving, unseeing eyes and would notice nothing around her. She knew many poems by heart, all of *The Demon* and *Eugene Onegin* from the first line to the last; but she didn't really share Father's taste for German philosophy and sociology—she found these less interesting than the rest. I never saw popular novels such as those by Verbitsky or Artsybashev in our house; it seems that both Father and Mother were of one mind in their contempt for these. It was I who brought home the first one of this kind; Father was no longer living then, and I was a student in the fourth grade, and the book that I accidentally left in the dining room was called *A Woman in the Middle*. Mother accidentally saw it and when I returned home in the evening she asked me, disgustedly lifting the title page of the book with two fingers:

"You're reading this? What good taste you've got."

I was ashamed to the point of tears; forever afterwards this memory of Mother finding out about my short-lived weakness for pornographic and stupid novels was for me the most humiliating memory; if she had been able to tell my father about this, I don't believe I would have endured the unhappiness.

Mother loved Father with all her strength, all her soul. She didn't cry when he died, but both Nanny and I were afraid to be left alone with her. For three months, from early in the morning until late at night, she paced the living room from one corner to the other, without stopping. She spoke to no one, ate almost nothing, slept three or four hours a day and did not go out. The relatives were certain that she would lose her mind. I remember waking up one night in the nursery and hearing the quick steps along the carpet; I fell asleep, then woke up and once again heard the same barely audible shoes creaking and Mother's quick steps. I got out of bed and, barefoot and in my nightgown, went into the living room. "Mama, go to sleep. Mama, why are you walking around all the time?" Mother stared straight at me: I saw a pale, strange face and frightening eyes.

"Mama, I'm scared. Mama, go lie down a little."

She sighed as though coming to herself. "All right, Kolya, I'll go lie down now. Go to sleep."

In the beginning Mother's life had been a happy one. My father gave all his time to the family, leaving it only to go hunting and to do his scientific work, and nothing else interested him; he was remarkably courteous with women. He never argued with them, agreeing even when they said something completely at odds with his own views. But in general it seemed he couldn't fathom why other women existed on the earth at all. Mother said to him:

"You called Vera Mikhailovna 'Vera Vladimirovna' again. She's probably offended. How could you still not remember her name? Really, she's been with us for two years."

"Is that right?" Father said in surprise.

"Which one is she, the wife of the engineer who whistles?"

"No, the one that whistles is Darya Vasilievna and the engineer sings. But Vera Mikhailovna has nothing to do with them. She's the wife of a doctor, Sergei Ivanovich."

"But of course," Father said, growing animated, "I know her quite well."

"Yes, but first you called her 'Vera Vasilievna' and then 'Vera Petrovna', but her name is Vera Mikhailovna."

"Astonishing," Father said. "Of course, I was mistaken. Now I completely remember. I know this woman very well. She seems extremely nice and her husband is nice, too; but his pointer, on the other hand, isn't much of a pointer."

There were never any disagreements or quarrels at our home and everything went smoothly. But fate did not spoil Mother for long. First my older sister died; her death occurred as a result of a bath taken too soon after a stomach operation. Then, several years later, Father died and finally, during the Great War, my younger sister, a nine-year-old girl, passed away from a virulent strain of scarlet fever. She was sick for only two days. Mother and I became a twosome. She lived nearly in seclusion; I was left to myself and grew up in freedom. She could not forget the losses that had befallen her so suddenly, and for many years she lived as if under a spell, even more silent and immobile than before. She was remarkable for her excellent health and she never took ill; only in her eyes, which I remembered as being bright and indifferent, did there appear such a profound sorrow that when I looked into them, I became ashamed of the fact that I was alive. Later on my mother and I grew somewhat closer: I learned of the unusual strength of her love for the memory of my father and sisters, and her sad love for me. I learned as well that she was endowed with a flexible and quick imagination which considerably surpassed mine, and an ability to understand things which I never would have suspected. Furthermore, her superiority, which I had felt since childhood, was only further confirmed when I neared adulthood. I also understood one other thing, the most important thing: that the world of my second existence which I had thought to be closed forever and to everyone was known to my mother.

The first time I was separated from my mother for any length of time was the year I became a cadet. The military school was in another city: I remember the blue-white river, the green shrubbery of Timofeev, and the hotel where Mother took me for two weeks before the exams and where she taught me French grammar from a small textbook—I was weak in spelling. Then came the exams, goodbyes with Mother, a new uniform and full dress coat with shoulder-straps, and a driver in a torn coat who pulled incessantly on the reins and took Mother down to the train station, where she was to catch the train home. I was left alone. I kept my distance from the cadets, wandered for hours along the resonant halls of the school, and it was only later I remembered that I had far-away Christmas and two-weeks' leave to look forward to. I didn't like the military school. My peers differed from me in many things: Mostly they were children of officers, coming from a quasi-warlike milieu which I had never known; there had never been anyone from the military in our house, as Father steered clear of them with animosity and scorn. I could not get used to "Yes, Sir" and "No, Sir," and I remember that in answer to an officer's reprimand I said, "You're partly right, Colonel Sir," for which they punished me even more. I soon became friends with the cadets, however; but the authorities didn't like me even though I was a good student. Teaching methods at the school were quite diverse. One German man forced the whole class to read out loud, and thus along with the text of the German reader could be heard cocks crowing, the singing of indecent songs and yelping. The teachers were bad; no one distinguished himself, with the exception of the natural history teacher, a civil general and sarcastic old man who was a materialist and skeptic.

"What is hydroscopic wadding, Your Excellency?"

And he would answer, "Well, if a young cadet like you were to run into the courtyard and bleed like a calf and accidentally cut his tail, then you'd wrap wadding around his wound. You do this so that the cadet, who looks like a calf, won't be in too much pain. Do you understand?"

"Yes Sir, Your Excellency."

"Yes Sir," he muttered, smiling gloomily. "Ah, you . . ."

I don't know why I found this civil general so utterly delightful. When he turned his attention towards me I was very happy. Once I had to answer a lesson which I knew quite well and I said "for the most part," "primarily" and "in essence" several times. He looked at me with a cheerful smirk and gave me a good grade.

"What an educated cadet. 'For the most part' and 'in essence'. In essence, you may go to your seat."

Another time he stopped me in the corridor, made a serious face and said, "I would ask you, Cadet Sosedov, not to wag your tail around so much when you walk. It only attracts attention."

And he left, smiling just with his eyes. He was a unique teacher, unlike any of the other teachers in the school—just as the only thing I learned there was the art of walking on my hands. Later, after much time had passed since I had left the school, whenever I took it into my head to stand on my hands I would immediately see before me the recreation room's wax parquet floor, a dozen legs walking around my arms and the beard of my class preceptor: "Today you'll go without sweets again."

He always spoke in diminutives and this inspired an unconquerable disgust in me. I didn't like people who used diminutive words in an ironic sense; there is nothing more petty or base in a language. I noticed that these expressions are used most often either by insufficiently cultured people or simply by very evil people invariably swollen with human baseness. My class preceptor's presence was unpleasant in itself. But what I found especially distressing about school was that I could not suddenly get fed up with everything and go home; home was far away, in another city, twenty-four hours by train. Winter, the huge, dark building of the military school, the long, badly-lit corridors, the solitude; I felt weighed down and bored. I didn't want to study; it was forbidden to lie in bed. We amused ourselves by roller-skating along the newly waxed floors; we would leave the faucets in the washroom on all night; we jumped over stools and podiums, and took countless bets on the meatballs, the dessert, the sugar and the macaroni. We were all rather mediocre students, with the exception of the first in the class, Uspensky, who was the most diligent and unhappy cadet among us. He crammed with a frenzy; he prepared his lessons all the time, from dinner until ten o'clock when he went to bed. In the evening he would spend an hour and a half on his knees in silence, sobbing inaudibly.

The son of very poor parents, he studied on a scholarship and had to receive good grades.

"What are you praying for, Uspensky?" I asked, waking up and seeing his body in a long night shirt in front of the small ikon on his pillow. He slept two beds away from me.

"I'm praying that I may study," he quickly answered in his usual speaking voice, then continued in a frenzy:

"Our Father! Who art in Heaven . . ." Moreover, he didn't understand the words to the prayer very well and pronounced "who art" as if it meant "since you are."

"You don't pray right, Uspensky," I said to him. "You need to say 'Our Father who art in Heaven' all together."

He suddenly broke off praying and began to cry.

"What's wrong with you?"

"Why are you bothering me?"

"Go ahead and pray, I'll leave you alone." And once again it was quiet, the beds, the smoking night lamps, the darkness beneath the ceiling and the small white figure on his knees. In the morning the drums thundered, a horn played beyond the wall, and the officer on duty passed by each bed.

"Reveille, get up."

I never could get used to military language. At home a pure and correct Russian was spoken, and military expressions hurt my ears. Once I saw the company register in which someone had written, "Issued a certain quantity of cloth for the purpose of constructing coats," and, further on, something about expenditures for "glazing" the windows. Two of my comrades and I discussed these expressions and decided that the officer on duty—we were sure it was he who wrote them—was an uneducated man; and this was hardly far from the truth, although we didn't really know the officer on duty that day. It was known only that he was an extraordinarily religious man. The school was very strict when it came to religion: Every Saturday and Sunday they took us to church, and this walk, which no one could evade, was responsible for my coming to hate the Orthodox service. Everything about it offended me: the greasy hair of the fat deacon who blew his nose at the altar and who, before he began his service, quickly tweaked his nose and cleared his throat with a short cough, and only then would his deep bass quietly bellow forth:

"Bless us O Lord!" And the priest's thin little ridiculous voice that answered from beyond the closed tsarist gates, with their pasted-on gold icons and poorly-drawn angels with melancholy faces and fat lips:

"Blessed kingdom of the Father, the Son and the Holy Ghost, now and everlasting and for all time . . ."

And the long-legged regent with the tuning fork who sang while listening to the singing of the others at the same time, and because of this his face expressed unbelievable strain; I found all of this absurd and superfluous, although I did not always understand why. But as I studied the Ten Commandments and read the Gospels I thought, "What kind of Christian is our lieutenant-colonel, continually punishing me the way he does, standing me under the clock, leaving me "without sweets." Is that really what Christ taught? I addressed Uspensky, the resident expert on the Commandments.

"What do you think?" I asked. "Is our lieutenant-colonel a Christian?"

"Of course," he said quickly, taken aback.

"Then what right does he have to punish me every day?"

"Because you behave badly."

"Then why does it say in the Gospels, 'Judge not and you shall not be judged?'"

"And you shall not be judged, that's the passive voice," Uspensky whispered to himself as if verifying his knowledge. "That was not referring to a cadet."

"Then to whom?"

"I don't know."

"That is, you don't understand the Commandments," I said and left, and my hostile attitude toward religion and to the school grew even stronger.

Much later on after I'd already become a student at the gymnasium, I remembered the military school like a heavy, stony dream. It still continued to exist somewhere deep within me; I remembered particularly well the smell of the wax on the parquet floor and the taste of meatballs with macaroni, and as soon as I smelled anything reminding me of the school I would instantly imagine the huge dark hall, the night lamps, the dormitory, the long nights and the morning drum, Uspensky in his white night shirt and the lieutenant-colonel, who was a bad Christian. That life had been difficult and barren; the memory of the stony, torpid school was an unpleasant one, like that of a barracks or prison or a long sojourn in a godforsaken place in a cold railway hut somewhere between Moscow and Smolensk, lost in the snow, in the deserted, frosty expanse.

Nonetheless, the early years of my schooling were the hap-

piest, most carefree years of my life. In the beginning—in the
military school as well as the gymnasium where I was later to
enroll—I was disturbed by the sheer number of my classmates.
I didn't know how to relate to all of these short-haired boys. I
had become used to the fact that several lives existed around
me—Mother, Sister, Nanny—people who were close to me and
who I knew; but such a mass of new and unknown people was
difficult for me to grasp all at once. I was afraid of losing myself
in this crowd, and the instinct for self-preservation which usually
remained asleep inside me suddenly awoke and provoked a series
of changes in my character which, most likely, would not have
occurred in another situation. I often ended up saying just the
opposite of what I had been thinking and would act just the way
I wasn't supposed to; I became impudent, lost the slowness of
movement and response which completely reigned at home after
Father's death, as if I had been spellbound by Mother's cold
magic. It was difficult for me to snap out of the habits I had acquired at school, although I soon learned the art of doing this. I
unconsciously understood that one must not be the same with
all people; so, after a brief period of minor domestic disorder, I
once again became the obedient boy in the family; at school my
short temper was caused by my being punished more than the
other boys. Although I was the least talented member of my family, I still inherited some of my mother's good memory, but my
perception was never spontaneously conscious, and only after
some time would I understand the full sense of whatever had
been explained to me. Father's abilities came through to me in
quite an altered form: In place of his strong will and patience, I
had stubbornness; instead of hunting prowess, sharp sight, physical indefatigability and precise powers of observation. I directly
inherited only his unusual, blind love for the living world and
the strained but involuntary and pointless interest in everything
that happened around me, in all that was said and done. I studied very reluctantly but got good grades; it was my behavior
alone that continually served as a topic of conversation in ped-
agogical meetings. They attributed my behavior to the fact that
I never felt the fear children have around teachers and that I

never concealed my feelings towards them. My class preceptor complained to Mother that I was vulgar and impudent, although my development was almost exceptional for my age. Mother, who got called to school rather frequently, would say, "Excuse me, but it seems to me that you must not really understand the art of handling children. At home Kolya is a very quiet boy and is not at all rowdy and usually not impudent, either."

And she would send the attendant for me. I'd go into the receiving room and greet her; after speaking with me for ten minutes she'd let me go.

"Yes," agreed the class preceptor, "his tone is entirely different with you. I don't know how you manage it. In class he's quite unbearable," and he would spread his hands offendedly. Both the class preceptor and the inspector especially blamed me for my insolence with the history teacher (I once had the following conversation with him: "Who is Konrad Vallenrod?" I had asked, since I'd read his name in a book and didn't know him. After thinking it over he said, "He is a hooligan just like you"), who would stand me in the corner for "not sitting quietly." I wasn't really so guilty: My neighbor had run an eraser over my head—something the teacher did not see—and I had hit him in the chest-something which he did. I could not betray my friend, so in response to the historian's words, "Go stand at the wall; you can't behave yourself," I fell silent. The historian, accustomed to my continual retorts and not hearing them this time, suddenly got mad at me, started yelling, and hit his stool against the floor; but as he did so he made some kind of clumsy movement, slipped, and fell right off the podium. The class didn't dare laugh. I said, "That served you right. I'm delighted you fell."

He was besides himself with rage, ordered me to leave the class and go to the inspector. But later on, as he was a good man, he calmed down and forgave me, although I hadn't asked for his forgiveness. Usually he treated me without malice; my real enemy was the class preceptor, the Russian teacher who couldn't stand me just as he could not stand any equal. Even so, he was unable to give me bad grades since I knew Russian better than anyone in the class. On the other hand, I would end up going "without lunch" practically every day. I remember the endlessly sad feeling with which I watched the others go home after the last class. The first to leave were those who could get their things together quickly, then the others and finally the slowest, and I would remain alone, looking at the mysterious, silent map that reminded me of the lunar landscapes in my father's books; on the blackboard there was a stained piece of cambric rag and a deformed drawing of a devil made by Paramonov, the best student in the art class, and I thought that this little devil somehow resembled the artist Sipovsky. This tedium would continue for about an hour until the class preceptor returned: "Go home and try not to behave like such a hooligan."

Awaiting me at home were dinner and books, and the evening game in the courtyard, which was supposed to be off limits.

At that time we were living in a house belonging to Alexei Vasilievich Voronin, a former officer who came from a long line of nobility, a strange and wonderful man. He was tall with a thick moustache and beard that hid his face: His bright, angry eyes, I remember, always used to embarrass me. For some reason I felt that this man knew things about me which should never be told. He was horrible when in a rage, would forget himself and could easily end up shooting someone: The many months of the Port Arthur siege had taken its toll on his nervous system. He gave the impression of being a man who harbored silent strength. But for all this he was kind, although he spoke to children in an invariably severe tone, was never moved by them and never called them affectionate names. He was educated and intelligent and possessed an ability, almost never found in the average person, to understand abstract ideas and remote feelings. This man understood more than a retired officer needed to in order to live a happy life. He had a son who was four years my senior and two daughters, Marianna and Natalya, one my age and the other the same age as my sister. The Voronins were my second family. Alexei Vasilievich's wife, a German by origin and an eternal defender of the guilty, was known for her inability to turn down any request made of her

"Ekaterina Genrikhova, could I ask you for some bread and jam. You know, the jam you made for New Year's?"

"What do you mean, my dear?" she said, horrified. "That jam can't be touched."

"But Ekaterina Genrikhova, I want it so much, couldn't you possibly?" "Ah, you are I strange one. Well, I'll give you another English jam which is also very good . . ."

"Ekaterina Genrikhova, I know that one's no good. It smells of tar. Couldn't I have the one for New Year's?"

"You don't understand the simplest things. Well, hand me the bread, I'll bring it all to you."

Such hearty and healthy blood flowed in her veins that for many years she didn't change at all and, it appeared, was unable to grow old: She reached twenty-five and stayed that way her entire life. Under no circumstances did she lose her constant, peaceful toil, never forgot anything, and never worried. Once when there was a fire in the courtyard—the courtyard shed had caught on fire, and I woke up because everything around me was brightly lit by the flames and my windowpane was cracking from the heat—I saw Ekaterina Genrikhovna standing by my bed, dressed just as if everything were happening in the daytime, her hair in place, and calm.

"I'm sorry that it woke you," she said. "You were sleeping so sweetly. Well, you'd better get up in case, God forbid, the house should catch on fire. Don't fall back asleep—I still have to go and wake up your mother. All this happens because people treat fire so carelessly."

At the time her son was already in the fourth grade at school. He was a sweet boy but extremely dissolute and unbalanced. My mother greatly disliked his piano playing, although he was musically gifted; he pounded on the keyboard with such fury and pressed the pedal so mercilessly that she would say, "Misha, why are you using so much energy?"

And he would answer, "Because I'm so carried away."

We nicknamed the younger daughter of the Voronin family Sophie, since she was so much like the heroine of a book we had read called *Les Malheurs de Sophie*. This girl had a love for unusual adventures: She would dash off to the bazaar and wander around all day long among traders, pickpockets and thieves—people in good suits with wide-legged trousers—knife grinders, booksellers, butchers and those vendors of rubbish who exist, it seems, in all cities across the globe, who all dress in the same black rags; speak many languages badly and trade the kind of debris that not a soul needs; and nonetheless they live and generations change in their families, as if fate itself had destined them for just that trade and they could never be anything else; in my eyes they personified a magnificent immutability—or she'd rake off her stockings and shoes and go barefoot in the garden after it had rained, and returning home would boast:

"Mama, look, I've got black legs."

"Your legs certainly are quite black, only what's so good about that?"

The older daughter, Marianna, was known for her taciturn nature, her precocious femininity and her unusual firmness of character. Once, when she was eleven, her father called her a fool in one of those fits of rage that forced him to lose his usual politeness. She paled and said:

"I'm not going to speak to you from now on."

And she didn't speak to him for two years. She treated her sister and brother as if she were an adult; her family was not so much afraid of her as they were wary. All the children were beautiful in a good, robust way, physically strong and inclined to gaiety; but they were not the full-blown Russian sanguine type, thanks to the mother's German blood.

The Voronins and I made up only part of the society of children who met in the evening in the garden or courtyard of the Voronin's house; there were a few other boys and girls who joined us: the small, beautiful Jewish girl, Silva, who later became an actress; the twelve-year-old twins Valya and Lalya, forever at each others' throats; and the realist Volodya, who died soon after of diphtheria. While it was still light out, everybody played a kind of hopscotch where they would jump in a square drawn on the ground; these squares ended in a big uneven circle within which "Heaven" was written, and then, in a smaller circle,

"Hell." When it had grown dark we would begin a game of hide-and-seek and disperse for home only after the maid had called us at least three times. I divided my time between reading, school, and staying at home in the courtyard, and there were long periods of time when I would forget about that world of inner existence where I had once lived. Once in a while I would return to it—this was usually preceded by a sickly stare, irritability and a bad appetite—and I would notice that my second existence, endowed as it was with a gift for innumerable conversions and possibilities, was hostile to the first and was to grow more hostile as the former became enriched with new knowledge and grew stronger. It was as if my second existence were afraid of its own destruction, something which would happen when outwardly I grew definitively stronger. At those times I would perform silent, obscure work, attempting to achieve a completeness and a union of the two different lives, as I had succeeded in doing when I realized the necessity of being tough at school and gentle at home. But in this case I didn't feel I had the strength for what was actually a simple game. Besides which, I liked my inner life better than others. I noticed that in general my attention was more often attracted by those subjects which should not have affected me, while it remained indifferent to a great deal that directly concerned me. Usually much time would have to pass before I would understand the sense of a particular event, and only after it had completely lost any influence on my receptiveness would it acquire that meaning which it should have had when it took place. First it would migrate to a distant and illusory region to which my imagination descended only rarely, and where I would find, as it were, a geological stratification of my history. Things that rose up before me silently fell back down, and once again I would have to begin from the beginning, and only after I had experienced a severe shock and sunk to the bottom of consciousness would I come across fragments in which I had, at one time, lived, the ruins of cities which I had abandoned. This absence of spontaneous or quick recall of anything that happened to me, this impossibility of immediately knowing what do do, was later to cause me profound unhappiness, and was responsible for the mental catastrophe which took place soon after my first meeting with Claire. But this was somewhat later.

For a long time I didn't understand my attacks of fatigue, those days when I had done nothing and had no reason to be tired. But as I was getting into bed I would feel as if I had labored for many hours on end. Later I surmised that there were laws of internal movement which I didn't know and which forced me to bear a continual search for and pursuit of something which only fleetingly appeared before me in the shape of a huge, formless mass that looked like an underwater monster—it would appear and then vanish. Physically this exhaustion manifested itself in headaches and also, occasionally, a strange pain in the eyes, as if someone were pressing on them with their fingers. And not for one minute did the muffled, silent struggle going on in the depths of my consciousness cease, a struggle in which I myself hardly figured. I would often lose myself; I was not something defined once and for all. I would change, becoming first larger, then smaller, and perhaps this infidelity on the part of my own appearance, which did not allow me to split definitively into two separate beings, did allow me in reality to be more diverse than would have seemed possible.

These first, carefree years of life at the gymnasium were only rarely aggravated by those emotional crises from which I suffered so greatly but in which I nonetheless found an agonizing satisfaction. I lived happily—if one can live happily when a persistent shadow floats behind one's shoulders. Death was never far away, and the abyss into which my imagination plunged me seemed to belong to it. I think this feeling was hereditary: It was not for nothing that my father so violently detested everything that reminded him of the inevitable end; this fearless man felt his weakness here. It was as though my mother's unconscious, cold indifference reflected someone's final stillness, and the ravenous memories which my sisters possessed absorbed everything into themselves so quickly because, somewhere in their distant foreboding, death already existed. Occasionally I dreamed that I had died, that I was dying, that I would die; I could not scream, and I became surrounded by the usual silence which I had known for so long; suddenly it would spread out and change, taking on a new meaning I had not known until then: It was warning me. All my life, even when I was a child, it seemed to me that I knew a secret which others did not know; this strange delusion never left me. It could not have been based on external facts—I was no more or less educated than the rest of my ignorant generation. It was a feeling independent of my will. Very rarely, in the most trying moments of my life, I would experience an instantaneous, almost physical rebirth and approach my blind knowledge, this unreal comprehension of the miraculous. But then I would come to; I would be sitting in the same place, white and drained, and just as before everything surrounding me would hide in its stony, rigid forms, and objects would resume their perpetual and inaccurate appearance to which my sight had become accustomed.

After going through such a state I would forget all about it for a long time and I'd return to my daily cares and, if it were summer, to packing for my departure—because every year during vacation I went to the Caucasus, where many of my father's relatives lived. There, leaving the house of my grandfather which was on the outskirts of the city, I would go into the mountains. Eagles flew high up in the sky and I would walk through the tall grass with my Monte Cristo rifle, which I used to shoot sparrows and cats; across the way the Terek flowed noisily, and a lonely black mill rose up above its dirty waves. Far away, in the mountains, the snow glistened—and once again I would remember the snowdrift which I had seen near Minsk several years before. I went into the woods and lay down near the first anthill I came across, caught a caterpillar and carefully put it down by one of the entrances of the tall, porous pyramids from which ants were scurrying. The caterpillar crawled, pulling its twisting, hairy body into itself. It was overtaken by an ant; he snatched it by the tail and tried to stop it but the caterpillar easily dragged the ant behind him. Other ants came running to the aid of the first; they clung to the caterpillar from all sides. The living ball slowly inched its way back and finally disappeared into one of the openings. The same fate befell some large flies with blue wings, earth-

worms, and even beetles, although the latter were the most difficult for the ants to handle: The smooth, hard beetles were not
easy to capture. But I observed the cruelest struggle the time I led
a tarantula over to the anthill. I had never seen a fiercer creature,
even among wild beasts or insectivores famous for their cruelty—
if one could call such uncomprehending instinct cruelty. The most
cunning beasts I encountered were polecats, hamsters and
weasels, animals that generally possess certain analytical abilities
and in case of danger attack their enemy only if there is no possibility of escape. Only once did I see a weasel clinging to the
hand of a stableman who had wounded it with a stone; usually
weasels would run away with splendid, cunning speed. The tarantula never retreats. I carefully let him out of his glass dome: He
pounced on the anthill. The ants immediately fell upon him. He
moved along the ground in leaps and fought desperately. Soon
most of the ants were beaten and lay struggling on the ground,
dying. He furiously attacked anything that stirred, not availing
himself of his ability to flee, and stood in place as if awaiting new
adversaries. The battle lasted over an hour but in the end, even
the tarantula was drawn into the anthill. I watched this battle
with agonizing excitement, and vague, infinitely long-forgotten
memories dawned in the haze of my eternally buried knowledge.
Just after this I set off to catch lizards and pour water in gopher
holes. After a long wait, a little wet beast surfaced on the water;
he quickly jumped out, scurried off to one side and disappeared
in some other hole. But neither the weasel nor the lizard, the ants
nor even the tarantula were anything compared to the unusual
sight I happened upon early one July morning. I saw rats as they
were migrating. They traveled in a lopsided quadrangle, dragging
their tails along the ground and moving their paws up and down.
I was sitting in a tree and watching how quickly the ground
turned black, how the rats reached a small ravine and disappeared into it, and then once again they appeared, squeaking and
pushing onwards; I watched as they reached the Terek and their
pack stopped for a minute and then, having swum across the
river, disappeared into someone's garden. I got down from the
tree and went to lie by the edge of the woods.

The quiet, the sun, the trees . . . occasionally one could hear the sound of earth as it fell into the ravine and the crackle of small, dry branches—a wild boar running. I would fall asleep in the grass and wake up with a damp back and yellow fire in front of my eyes. Then, looking back at the red setting sun I would go home to the cool rooms of Grandfather's lodgings and would get there just in time to see the shepherd in his white felt hat driving the herd from the pasture; and Grandfather's bucking cows, known for their mean temper and good yield of milk, mooing as they passed through the gates of the cattle yard. I knew that the calves would immediately leap to their mothers, that the milkmaid would push their stubborn heads away from their mothers' udders, and that resilient jets of milk would ring as they streamed down onto the white bottoms of the buckets-and Grandfather would watch from the gallery which overlooked the yard and tap his stick on the floor, and then he would become lost in thought, as if remembering something. And as it happens, he had much to remember. Once, a long time ago, he used to drive herds of horses from hostile tribes and sell them. At the time this was considered a daring thing to do, and such exploits were grounds for the most unanimous praise; all of this happened in the thirties and forties of the last century. I remembered Grandfather as a small old man in a Caucasian coat with a gold dagger. In 1912 he turned one hundred; but he was strong and cheerful, and old age had made him kind. He died in the second year of the war riding an unbroken English horse, which was owned by his son, my father's older brother; but the incomparable art of riding, for which he'd long been famous, betrayed him. He fell from the horse, struck a sharp piece of copper lying on the ground, and died a few hours later. He knew and understood much, but did not talk about everything: Only from the words of other old men, his younger friends, was I able to find out that Grandfather had been sharp and cunning as a snake, as the simple-hearted people of the mid-nineteenth century put it. Grandfather's cunning surfaced when, after the Russians came to the Caucasus, he ceased his herding once and for all and took up a peaceful life which couldn't have been foreseen of this irrepressible man. All his friends perished, victims of revenge; his house was attacked twice, but the first time he learned about it ahead of time and left with his family. The second time he fired back from a rifle for several hours, killed six men and held out until help arrived. The attackers still managed to cause Grandfather some harm—they cut down his best apple tree. Grandfather was proud of his garden and no one was allowed to go there except me. "White-ripened" apples, huge golden plums and unusually large oval pears grew in this garden, and among them, in the depths of a ravine which in Caucasian Russian is called a gully, flowed a brook teeming with trout. I gorged myself on unripe fruit and went around with a pale face and suffering in my eyes. My aunt said to Grandfather reproachfully:

"You see that, you're the one who let the boy into the garden!"

It was actually my aunt who governed over all matters, and as Grandfather aged more and more, she gradually took power into her own hands. But usually she didn't dare contradict Grandfather and when she said, "You see that, you're the one who let him into the garden," Grandfather became enraged and cried in his high pitched, senile voice:

"Shut up!"

She was frightened half to death, went to her room and lay down on the sofa for a whole hour, her face buried in the pillow. Why are you so afraid?" I asked. "You don't know anything," my aunt answered. "Grandfather will kill me. Grandfather is a horrible man." "You're simply a coward," I said. "Grandfather is very nice and he wouldn't lay a finger on you even though you're mean and stingy. Why is it you don't want me to go into the garden?" I continued, forgetting about Grandfather and suddenly becoming annoyed. "You want all the apples for yourself? You wont eat them all anyway." "I'm going to write your mother and tell her how insolently you've spoken to me." But my aunt's threat didn't frighten me in the least, especially since I rarely argued with her—I was too busy shooting sparrows, hunting cats, and wandering in the woods. And, after having lived at Grandfather's for a month or month and a half, I would go on to Kislovodsk, which I loved dearly. It was the only provincial city that had metropolitan customs and an urban appearance. I loved its summer villas raised above the streets, its tiny park, its green vine of grapes that stretched from the station to the center of town, the noise of footsteps on the Kursaal gravel, and the carefree people who gathered there from all corners of Russia. But beginning with the first years of the war, Kislovodsk became flooded with ruined ladies, destitute artists and young people from Moscow and Petersburg; these young people went riding on hired horses and shook their elbows frantically, as if someone were nudging their arms from underneath. In Kislovodsk I would drink Narzan diluted with syrup, walk in the park and climb the mountain where, high above the city, stood a small white building with columns, called "The Temple of Air." I didn't know to whom this pretentious name, worthy of a town bard with long hair and three years of higher elementary school to his credit, belonged. But I loved to go up there; like a river of air the wind babbled and streamed between the columns. The white walls were covered with those inscriptions which have been perfected by Russian hopeless love and the vainglorious yearning to immortalize one's name. I loved the red stones on the mountain, loved even the "Castle of Perfidy and Love," where there was a restaurant which served wonderful trout. I loved the red sand of Kislovodsk's paths and the white beauties of Kursaal, the Northern women with the crimson whites of their rabbit eyes. I would walk in the park past a little cliff at Olkhovka, where a photographer was always on duty taking pictures of the women and young ladies standing above the falling wall of water; I saw these pictures everywhere, in the most remote corners of Russia.

"And this is a picture of me taken in Kislovodsk."

"Yes, yes," I would say "I know."

When I remember the Kislovodsk of my childhood I remember a white building with sensuous inscriptions. But the evenings were already beginning to grow cooler; in the early fall I would return home, to sink once more into that cold and tranquil life which in my mind is inextricably linked with crunchy snow, quiet rooms, soft carpets and plush living room sofas. At home it felt as if I had moved to some foreign country where one had to live differently from everywhere else. In the evening I loved to sit in my room with the light off; the rose-colored nocturnal blaze of the streetlamps reached my window in gentle reflections. The armchair was soft and comfortable, and in the apartment of the doctor who lived below the piano played slowly and haltingly. I felt as if I were sailing in the sea and foam, white as snow, was fluttering on the waves in front of me. And when I came to recall this time, it occurred to me that I had never gone through an adolescence. I had always sought the society of those older than myself and at twelve I tried in every way possible to appear grown up in spite of my obvious youth.

At thirteen I studied the *Treatise on Human Nature* by Hume and voluntarily went through the entire history of philosophy, which I found in our bookcase. This study invested me for all time with the habit of taking a critical stance towards everything; it served as a substitute for my insufficient quickness of perception and my unresponsiveness to external events. My feelings could not keep pace with my reason. The sudden love of change that came upon me in fits drew me magnetically away from home; there was a time when I would go our early, return late and frequent the company of questionable people—my billiard partners—playing a game which I surrendered to, at age thirteen and a half, for several weeks before the Revolution. I remember the thick gray smoke above the felt, and the players' faces protruding from the shadows: Among these shadows were people without profession, clerks, brokers and profiteers. I had several friends like myself and, after we all had won, we would set off at ten in the evening for the circus to watch the female riders, or to some cabaret, where music hall players sang obscene limericks and danced; they danced standing on a platform and folding their hands below the waist, so that the end of the thumb and index finger of the left hand touched the end of the same of the right. This striving for change and pull from home coincided with a time which preceded a new epoch in my life. This new epoch had always been just on the point of occurring: The vague consciousness of its growing inevitability always existed within me but was scattered in thousands of pieces. It was as if I stood on the bank of a river, ready to throw myself into the water, but couldn't bring myself to do it, knowing even so that there would be no escaping. It was only a matter of time before I would sink into the water and swim, urged on by its even, powerful flow. It was the end of the spring of 1917; the revolution had come several months earlier; and finally, that summer, in the month of June, something happened which my life had been leading me toward and for which all that I had lived and understood until then was only trial and preparation. On a stuffy evening which had replaced an unbearably hot day, on the playing court of the "Eagle" gymnastic society, standing in my bathingsuit and shoes, naked to the waist and tired, I saw Claire sitting in the bleachers.

The next morning I came again to the courts to sunbathe, and I lay down on the sand, threw my arms beneath my head and gazed into the sky. The wind shook the pleats of my suit, which was a bit too big for me. The court was empty, except that in the shadow of the orchard adjacent to the neighboring house Grisha Vorobyov, a student and gymnast, was reading a novel by Marc Krinitsky. After half an hour of silence he asked me:

"Have you read Krinitsky?"

"No, I haven't."

"It's just as well you haven't." And once again Grisha fell silent. I shut my eyes and saw an orange haze intersected by green streaks of light. I must have fallen asleep for a few minutes because I didn't hear anything. Suddenly I felt a cold, light hand touching my shoulder. Above me a pure, feminine voice said, "Comrade gymnast, please don't sleep." I opened my eyes and saw Claire, whose name I did not know at the time. "I'm not sleeping," I answered. "Do you know me?" asked Claire.

"Yesterday evening I saw you for the first time. What's your name?"

"Claire."

"Oh, you're French," I said, feeling happy for no apparent reason. "Please, sit down; only there's sand here."

"I see," said Claire.

"And you, it seems, are working hard on your gymnastics and can even walk along the parallel bars on your hands. That's quite a sight."

"I learned that in military school."

She was silent for a moment. She had long, rose-colored nails and very white hands, a shapely, hard body and long legs with slender calves. "Do you have tennis courts here?" Her voice contained the secret of instantaneous charm, because it always seemed to be already familiar; I thought I had heard this voice somewhere before and had managed to forget and then remember it again. "I want to play tennis," she said, "and join the gymnastics society. Go on, entertain me. You're very ungracious."

"How should I entertain you?"

"Show me how you do gymnastics."

I grasped the horizontal bar and demonstrated everything I could, then did a flip in the air and once again sat down on the sand. Claire looked at me, keeping her hand above her eyes: The sun was shining very brightly.

"Very good; only one of these days you're going to break your neck. But don't you play tennis?"

"No."

"You answer so tersely," Claire remarked. "Apparently you're not used to talking with women."

"With women?" I said in surprise; the thought never crossed my mind that it was necessary to speak to women in some special way. One should be more polite with them, but nothing more. "But you're hardly a woman, you're a young lady."

"And do you know the difference between a woman and a young lady?" Claire asked and began to laugh.

"Yes."

"Who explained it to you? Your aunt?"

"No, I knew it myself."

"By experience?" Claire said, and at once burst out laughing.

"No," I said, blushing.

"My God, he's turning red," Claire cried and clasped her hands together. Hearing the noise, Grisha, who had been sleeping peacefully on top of Marc Krinitsky, woke up. He coughed and stood up: His face was puffy, a green stripe from the grass crossed his cheek:

"Who is this handsome and comparatively young man?"

"At your service," said Grisha in a deep voice, still hoarse and sounding of sleep. "Grigory Vorobyov."

"You say it so proudly, as if you were saying 'Lev Tolstoy!'"

"Friend of the president of this pleasant organization," Grisha explained, "and a student in the third year of the faculty of law."

"You forgot to add, 'and reader of Marc Krinitsky,'" I said.

"Don't pay him any attention," Grisha said, turning to Claire. "This youth is extraordinarily immature."

At that time I was between the fifth and sixth grades; Claire was finishing her tenth and last. She was not a regular inhabitant of our city: Her father, a merchant, occasionally lived in the Ukraine. All of them—that is, Claire's father and mother and her older sister—occupied an entire floor of a big boarding house and lived separately from one another. Claire's mother was never home; Claire's sister, a student at the conservatory, played the piano and walked around the city with a student named Yurochka always trailing behind her, carrying a folder filled with sheets of music. Her entire life consisted of these two activities— walking and playing; while at the piano she would say quickly without stopping, "My God, and to think I haven't gone out of the house today," and while walking, she would suddenly re- member that she hadn't sufficiently practiced some exercise or other; and Yurochka, always by her side, would only delicately cough and change the folder of music from one hand to the other. It was a strange family. The head of the household, a grey- haired man who was always meticulously dressed, seemed to ig- nore the existence of the boarding house in which he lived. He went to and from the city in his yellow automobile, went to the theater or a restaurant every night, and many of his acquain- tances didn't even suspect that he was raising two daughters and provided for his wife, their mother. Occasionally he would bump into her at the theater and would bow to her extremely courte- ously, and she would respond with such gentility that it seemed somewhat put on and even a bit mocking.

"Who is that?" the father's companion would ask.

"Who is that?" asked the man accompanying the wife.

"That's my wife."

"That's my husband."

And they would both smile and they both knew and saw he, his wife's smile; she, her husband's.

The daughters were left to their own devices. The older one hoped to marry Yurochka. The younger one, Claire, was indifferently receptive to everyone; there were no rules at home, no set hours for meals. I was in their apartment several times. I would go there directly from the court, tired and happy because I was with Claire. I loved her room with its white furniture, its big desk covered with green blotting paper—Claire never wrote anything—and a leather armchair with lion heads designed on the arms. There was a big white carpet with a portrait of an overly long-bodied horse with a lean rider looking like a yellowed Don Quixote; the low divan with its pillows was very soft and sloping; its incline faced the wall. I even loved the watercolor of Leda and the Swan that hung on the wall, although the swan was dark—no doubt a hybrid of a normal swan and an Australian swan, I said to Claire—but Leda was unforgivably out-of proportion. I loved the portraits of Claire—there were many of them, since Claire loved herself—not simply what was immaterial and individual, which all people love in themselves, but her body, her voice, her hands and her eyes as well. Claire was cheerful and mocking and knew, perhaps, far too much for her eighteen years. She would joke with me, force me to read humorous stories aloud, dress in men's suits, draw a moustache on her face with burnt cork and speak in a deep voice, demonstrating how a "proper youth" ought to behave. But notwithstanding Claire's jokes and that simplicity with which she always behaved around me, I did not always feel at ease. Claire was at that age when all a girl's strength, all the efforts of her coquettishness, each of her movements and every idea are unconscious manifestations of her ineluctible, budding sexuality—a force which is often almost impersonal and turns from the entanglements of mutual relations into something else, slips from our understanding and begins to carry on an independent life, just as an unseen plant in a room fills the air with an agonizing and irresistible smell. At the time, I didn't understand all of this but could not stop feeling it; and I was not well. My voice would crack, I would answer out of place, grow ashen and, looking at myself in the mirror, wouldn't even recognize my own face. It always seemed to me that I was sinking into a fiery and sweet liquid and seeing Claire's body and her bright eyes with their long lashes near me. It was as if Claire understood my state: She would sigh, stretching her entire body out on the divan—usually she would be sitting—and suddenly turn over on her back with a changed face and clenched teeth. This could have gone on for a long time had I not ceased going to Claire's after a while, having been offended by her mother. This happened quite unexpectedly. I was sitting, as always, at Claire's, in the armchair; Claire was lying on the divan. I heard a deep feminine voice irritably speaking to the maid. "My mother," said Claire. "That's strange, she's rarely home at this hour." And at that very moment Claire's mother came into the room without knocking. She was a lean woman of about thirty-four; a diamond necklace hung around her neck; there were huge emeralds on her fingers. She might have looked beautiful except that her face was spoiled by big lips and bright, cruel eyes. I stood up and bowed to her. Claire immediately introduced me. Having barely looked at me her Mother said, "Infinitely glad to meet you," while in the same breath addressing Claire in French:

"I don't know why you always invite young people like him over. This one's got his dirty shirt unbuttoned and doesn't even know how to conduct himself properly."

Claire blanched.

"This young man understands French quite well," she said.

Her mother looked at me reproachfully, as if I were guilty of something, and quickly left the room, noisily slamming the door behind her. Once in the hall she cried, "Oh, everyone leave me alone!"

After this occurrence I stopped going to Claire's; soon it was late autumn, tennis season was over, and I could no longer see

Claire on the courts. In answer to my letters Claire set up two rendezvous but didn't keep either of them, and I didn't see her for four months. By then it was already winter; in the woods outside of the city, where I go skiing, the trees jingled like silver from the frost; daredevils cruised along the glassy road to the country restaurant, The Varsal. Above the snowy plains which began just beyond the woods, ravens were slowly flying. I followed their leisurely flight and thought about Claire; and the strange hope of meeting her here suddenly began to seem possible, although there was no question that Claire could not come here. But because I was preparing myself for that meeting with her and forgetting all else, my ability to think reasonably was stifled; I resembled a man who, having lost his money, searches for it everywhere, especially where it could not possibly be. For those four months I thought of nothing but Claire. I kept seeing her small figure, her gaze, her feet in black stockings. I imagined the dialogue that would take place between us; I heard Claire's laughter. I saw her in my dreams and, slowly gliding forward on my skis, I would stare unthinkingly at the snow as if searching for her footprints. Having stopped in the woods to smoke a cigarette, I would listen to the crackle of the branches, bent under the weight of the snow, and wait, ready to hear her footsteps scattering the snowy dust, and in this white cloud I would see Claire. And although I knew her appearance quite well I would not always picture her the same way: She would change, taking on the forms of various women, sometimes becoming like Lady Hamilton, at other times like the fairy Rautendale. I didn't understand my state at the time; now, however, it seemed to me that all these oddities and changes were like a searchlight running along a wide, smooth strip of water, making the water ripple and shine. Someone looking at this would see a glimmering, broken representation of a sail and the light of a distant home, the white ribbon of a limestone highway and a shimmering fish tail or glittering image of some huge glass building in which he had never lived. I grew cold; I set out along the path once more, heading towards the city. It was already evening; snow, rose-colored from the sunset, was everywhere, and beyond the far curve of the highway bells jingled beneath the shaft bow of a harness, and their sounds, babbling indistinct melodies, clashed and interrupted one another. It was growing dark; and it was like blue glass thickening in the air, blue glass in which the image of the city where I was to return rose up and where, in a lofty white boarding house, Claire lived. I thought to myself that at that very moment she was lying on the divan, and that as always the silent, yellow Don Quixote was galloping on the carpet and the dark grey swan embraced the heavy Leda; and the path from Claire to myself stretched across the ground and instantly joined the woods through which I was walking with this room, this divan, and Claire, surrounded by romantic themes. I waited—and was deceived: And through these incessant mistakes Claire's black stockings, her laughter and her eyes united in an inhuman and bizarre image in which the fantastic was mixed with the real, and the memory of my childhood was mixed with the vague premonition of catastrophe; and this was so incredible that many times I wished that I were dreaming and could wake up. This state, in which I both was and was not suddenly came to take on familiar forms, and I recognized the white ghosts of my former wanderings within the unknown, and once again I lapsed into my former illness; all objects seemed incorrect and diffuse, and once again the orange flame of an underground sun illuminated the valley where I had fallen in a cloud of yellow sand onto the banks of a black lake, in my dead silence. I did not know how much time had passed before the moment I saw myself in bed, in a room with high ceilings. I was then measuring time by distance, and it seemed to me that I had walked on, endlessly, until someone's salutary will had stopped me. Once, while hunting, I saw a wounded wolf escaping from the dogs: He jumped heavily through the snow, leaving red tracks along the white field. He stopped frequently and each time would once again, with difficulty, attempt to run; and each time he fell I felt that a horrible terrestrial force was trying to rivet him to one place and hold him there—a flinching grey mass—until the bared teeth of the dogs drew near. "It is this same force," I thought, "which, like a huge magnet, rivets me in my mental wanderings and pins me to the bed"; and once again I could hear Nanny's weak voice reach me as if it were coming from another bank of an invisible blue river:

> Oh, I don't see my beloved
> In the village or in Moscow,
> I only see my beloved
> In the dark night, in a sweet dream.

On the wall there hangs the long-familiar portrait by Sipovsky, the rooster which he drew while I watched. "And at Claire's there is a Swan and Don Quixote," I think, and at that moment lift myself up. "Yes," I say to myself as if I had just awakened and begun to see clearly. "Yes, it's Claire. But what is 'it'?" I think anxiously once again and see that it is everything: Nanny, the rooster, the swan, Don Quixote, and myself, and the blue river which flows through the room— it' was all things surrounding Claire. She is lying on the divan with a white lace and clenched teeth, her breasts protrude beneath her white blouse, her black-stockinged legs swim in the air as if in water, and the fine veins under her kneecaps swell from the blood which courses through them. Beneath her—brown velvet, above her a stucco ceiling, around her—myself and the swan, Don Quixote and Leda languish within those forms which have been granted us forever; the houses surrounding Claire's hotel crowd us, beyond the city there are fields and woods, beyond the fields and woods—Russia; beyond Russia, high up in the sky, immobile, flies a capsized ocean, the wintry, arctic waters of space. And below, in the doctor's apartment, someone is playing the piano and the sounds rock back and forth as if on a swing. "Claire, I'm waiting for you," I said aloud. "Claire, I shall always be waiting for you." And once again I saw the pale face separated from its body and Claire's knees, as if a hand had severed them and was now showing them to me: "You wanted to see Claire's face? You wanted to see her legs? Look!" And I looked at this face as I would stare at a talking head in a wax museum, surrounded by wax figures in strange costumes, beggars, hoboes and killers. But why, I thought, are there all these fragments of myself and everything in which I lead so many existences—this crowd of people and the endless noise of sounds and all the rest: the snow, the trees, the houses, the valley with the black lake— why was all of this suddenly embodied within me, and I thrown onto the bed and condemned to lie for hours in front of the translucent portrait of Claire and to be this immobile fellow traveler of her's, to become, like Don Quixote and Leda, a romantic character, and after so many years to have lost myself once again, as in childhood, as before, as always. Even after my illness had passed I continued to live as if I were in a dark black well, above which Claire's pale face was continually rising up, changing and reflecting in the dark, watery mirror. The well swayed back and forth like a tree in the wind and Claire's reflection lengthened and spread out without end and, beginning to tremble, disappeared.

More than anything else I loved snow and music, when there had been a snowstorm and it seemed as if there was nothing, neither houses nor land, but only white smoke and wind and the rustle of air; when I crossed this moving expanse I occasionally thought that if the legend of the creation of the world had originated in the north, the first words of the Holy Book would have been: "In the beginning there was a snowstorm." And when it had subsided, suddenly the whole world appeared from beneath the snow, like a fairy-tale forest growing out of someone's cosmic desire: I saw the curved lines of the black buildings and the drift gathering with a whine and the small figures of people walking along the street. During a snowstorm I especially loved to watch birds as they flew through the snow, then perched on the ground. They would close and open their wings as if they didn't want to leave the air, but still they would land and immediately, as if by magic, turn into black lumps walking about on invisible legs. And they would raise their wings in uniquely "birdlike movements which, for some strange reason, I felt I understood. It had been a long time since I had believed either in God or in angels, but I retained a visual picture of the heavenly forces from my childhood; and I thought that those winged, beautiful people would not fly or sit like birds; they shouldn't make quick movements, for such flapping of wings betrays vanity. When I saw birds swooping down from a great height, it always reminded me of a killed eagle. I would remember how once Father, a rifle slung across his shoulder, returned from an unsuccessful wild boar hunt; I went up to greet him. I was about eight years old at the time. Father took me by the hand, looked up and said, "Look, Kolya, do you see the bird flying?"

"Yes."

"That's an eagle."

Very high up in the sky, with its wings spread open, an eagle truly soared; first bending to the side, then straightening out, it flew slowly, or so it seemed to me, above us. It was very hot and bright out.

"The eagle can look at the sun without blinking," I mused. Father aimed for a long time, following the eagle's flight with the sight of his gun, then fired. Up above the eagle instantly twitched as the bullet hit him in mid-air, beat his wings quickly a few times and then fell. He spun like a top on the ground and opened his dirty beak; his feathers were bloody.

"Don't go near him," Father cried to me as I rushed towards the very spot where the eagle had fallen. I approached the bird only after he had stopped moving. He lay on the ground, one half-open, crushed wing bent, his head with its bloodied beak bent forward and his yellow eyes already turning glassy. On one of his claws shone a copper ring with something scrawled on it.

"This eagle is an old one," Father muttered. I remembered this every time there was a snowstorm, because the first time I recalled the dead eagle was during a snowstorm; I was in a park at the time, on skis, and the storm had forced me to seek shelter in a small hut that stood in the woods on the outskirts of the city. Inside the hut there was a ski station. After waiting for the storm to pass, I went into the woods again: The skis sunk deep into the soft, freshly fallen snow. After a little while frozen rain began to fall, and the whole sky instantly reddened. "There will be wind," I thought, but then it grew quiet. "There will be wind," I repeated out loud. And just then far, far into the woods

I heard a noise. Was it a leaden icicle falling from a tree, or a light wind catching one of those translucent stalagtites which hung down over the firs? I didn't know. I knew only that afterwards it was quiet again and then once more I could hear the ice falling, as if a small forest dwarf living somewhere in the hollow of a tree was softly playing a glassy violin. And suddenly it appeared to me that a huge terrestrial expanse had rolled up like a geographical map, and that instead of Russia I had landed in the fairy-tale Black Forest. Beyond the trees woodpeckers were tapping away; the white, snowy mountains were falling asleep above the lake's frozen plains; and below, in a valley, a delicate, jingling net hardening into frost floated in the air. At that moment, as with every time I felt truly happy, I vanished from my own consciousness. This would happen in the woods, on a field, on a river or at the seashore; it would happen when I was reading a book which captivated me. Even then, I would feel only too strongly the imperfection and brevity of that silent concert which surrounded me wherever I was. It would pass through me, and along its path wonderful pictures, unforgettable smells, a city in Spain, dragons and beauties rose up and died away. I myself, however, remained a strange creature whose limbs were of no use to him, who bore upon his back a host of inconvenient and useless things. My life seemed to be someone else's. I loved my house and my family very much, but I often dreamed that I was walking in our city and, passing by the building where I lived, was unable to enter, for I felt the need to move on. Something forced me to strive onwards, as if I didn't know that I would fail to see anything new. I had this dream often. I carried within myself an endless number of ideas, feelings and images which I had experienced or seen, and I did not feel their weight. And when I thought about Claire, my body would fill up with molten metal and everything that I continued to think about— ideas, memories, books—all of these would inevitably hasten to drop their usual forms and Brehm's *The Life of Animals* or the dying eagle invariably turned into Claire's slender calves and knees, her blouse, through which the circular, agonizing spots surrounding her nipples could be seen, her eyes and face. I tried not to think about Claire, but only rarely succeeded. There were evenings, though, when I didn't think about her at all; or more accurately, when the idea of Claire lay in the depths of my awareness and it seemed to me that I had forgotten about her.

Once, very late at night, I was returning home on foot from a circus and wasn't thinking about Claire. It was snowing heavily; the cigar I was smoking kept going out. There was no one on the streets and all the windows were dark. I walked on and remembered a song one of the clowns had sung:

> I'm not Soviet,
> I'm not a cadet,
> Oh, I'm a people's commissar. . .

and that strange, unstable effect which is achieved when an artist plays some musical instrument and sings to the accompaniment of the motif, still reverberated in my ear. At the same time, I suddenly felt that something was about to happen. And then, thinking about it, I realized that I had been hearing footsteps behind me for some time. I turned around: Surrounded by the fox collar of her coat, as if in a yellow cloud, her eyes wide open as she gazed through the slowly falling snow, Claire was walking behind me. Not far from the corner I heard a quick gurgle of steaming water strike the sidewalk, then the banging of a hammer against a stone, and immediately afterwards there came the kind of silence which I would hear during attacks of my illness. It became difficult for me to breathe; a snowy fog was suspended in the air around me. And everything that happened from that moment on took place next to and apart from me; it was difficult for me to speak and Claire's voice came to me as if from far away.

"Hello, Claire," I said. "I haven't seen you for quite a long time."

"I was busy," answered Claire, laughing.

"I was getting married."

Claire is married now, I thought uncomprehendingly. But the awful habit of having to carry on the conversation at all costs somehow retained a small part of my slipping attention and I answered and spoke and even grieved all the while; but everything I said was false and did not correspond with my feelings. Still laughing and looking fixedly at me—and now I remembered how for a split second her pupils flashed with fright when she understood that she would not be able to draw me out of my sudden torpidity—Claire told me that she bad been married for nine months but that she didn't want to spoil her figure. "That's nice," I muttered, having understood only the sentence about Claire not wanting to spoil her figure; but I didn't hear, nor did I want to understand, the reason why her figure might have been spoiled. At another time this simple declaration of not wanting her figure spoiled would certainly have been surprising, just as it would be if someone were to say, "I don't want my leg to be cut off."

"You should reconcile yourself to the fact that I'm not a girl any more, that I have become a woman. Do you remember our first conversation?"

"Reconcile myself?" I thought, catching the word.

"Yes, I must reconcile myself . . ."

"I'm not angry with you, Claire," I said.

"It doesn't frighten you?" Claire continued. "No, on the contrary."

We were now walking together; I held Claire by the arm. Snow was falling all around us in heavy flakes.

"Write this down in French," I heard Claire's voice say, and it took me a second to remember who was speaking to me, "Claire was no longer a virgin."

"Very well," I said, "Claire was no longer a virgin." When we had reached Claire's hotel she continued, "My husband is out of town. My sister is sleeping at Yura's, and Mama and Papa aren't here either."

"You'll sleep peacefully, Claire."

But once again Claire began to laugh.

"I hope not."

Suddenly she came up to me and took me by the collar of my coat.

"Come home with me," she said sharply. Through the fog in front of me, at somewhat of a distance, I saw her immobile face. I didn't move. Her face came closer and grew irate.

"Have you gone mad or are you ill?"

"No, no," I said.

"What's the matter with you?"

"I don't know, Claire."

She didn't say goodbye, ascended the stairs, and I heard her open the door and stand at the threshold for a moment. I wanted to go after her and could not. The snow was still coming down as before and disappeared into thin air, and in this snow everything that I had known and loved until that moment swirled and disappeared with the snow. I didn't sleep for two nights after that. Some time later I met Claire again on the street and bowed to her, but she did not respond.

In the course of the ten years which separated my two meetings with Claire, nowhere, never could I forget this. At times I would regret that I had not died, and at others I would imagine myself as Claire's beloved. As a vagabond spending the night in the open air of barbaric Asiatic countries, I still remembered her irate face and, even after many years had gone by, I would wake up at night from a feeling of infinite regret, the reasons for which I did not immediately comprehend, and only later would I guess that the reason was the memory of Claire. Once again I would see her through the snow and storm, and the soundless crash of the greatest shock in my life.

I don't remember a time—regardless of the situation or whom I was with—when I was not certain that one far-off day I would live in a different place and in a different way. I was always ready for change, even though there were no changes to foresee, and I would feel somewhat sorry in advance to abandon that circle of friends and acquaintances to whom I had had time to grow accustomed. Sometimes I thought that this continual anticipation of mine did not depend on external circumstances, nor on a love for change; rather, it was something innate and indispensable and, perhaps, as vital as sight or hearing. However, the imperceptible connection between this anticipation and other impressions which came to me from without had always existed, but could not be explained through logical reasoning. I remember not long before my departure which, at the time, I had not yet decided upon, while sitting in a park, I suddenly heard next to me the strains of a Polish conversation; the words "wszystko" and "bardzo" were repeated over and over. I felt a chill up my spine and sensed a powerful certainty that now there could be no doubt that I would go away. What relation could these words possibly have had to the course of my life's events? But, hearing them, I understood that there was no longer any doubt. I didn't know if I would have been so certain had there been, instead of a Polish conversation next to me, the whistle of a thrush, or the melancholic voice of a cuckoo. At that moment I looked attentively at the man saying "wszystko" and "bardzo"; he was, apparently, a Polish Jew whose face expressed fright and a readiness to smile at the least provocation and also, perhaps, a barely perceptible, barely visible but nonetheless unmistakable baseness. Sycophants and gigolos have such faces. Sitting next to him was a girl of about twenty; she had rings on her reddened fingers, with their ragged, long nails, soured eyes and the kind of smile that would instantly make every man who happened to glance at her feel close to her. I never saw these people again; but I remembered them as well as if I had known them for a long time. Besides, unfamiliar people always interested me. Their distinctiveness consisted in that which, in familiar people, had become something ordinary, safe and therefore uninteresting. At the time it seemed to me that each stranger knew something I could not divine. I could tell the difference between simple unknowns from strangers par excellence, a type which existed in my imagination as a kind of foreigner that is not only a person of another nationality but someone who also belongs to another world, one which I did not have access to. Perhaps my feeling toward Claire arose in part because she was both French and a foreigner. And even though she spoke Russian absolutely fluently and purely, and understood everything down to the sense of popular proverbs, there remained in her a kind of charm which a Russian woman would not possess. Her French worked an unknown and wonderful charm upon my ear, despite the fact that I spoke French easily and, it would seem, should also have known its musical secrets—not as well as Claire, of course, but known them nonetheless. And, on the other hand, I always unconsciously craved the unknown, within which I hoped to find new possibilities and new lands; it seemed to me that from contact with the unknown everything that was important, all of my knowledge, strength and desire to understand more and more new things, would suddenly rise up and appear in a purer form; and, once having understood everything, I would thereby subordinate it to myself. It was this same striving, only in another form which, I thought at the time, had roused both knights and lovers; both the crusades and the lovers kneeling before foreign princesses were manifestations of the unquenchable desire for knowledge and power. But here a contradiction arose in the fact that there had been immediate causes for the knights' crusades, reasons which they themselves believed in and for which they went to war. And weren't these reasons the true ones and the others, only fabrications? All of history, Romanticism and art appeared only after the event which had served as the basis for their rise had already died and no longer existed, and everything we read and think about this event is only the play of the shadows which live in our imaginations. And, just as in childhood when I had invented my adventures on the pirate ship, the ones Father told me about, so too did I later create kings, conquistadors and beauties, forgetting that sometimes beauties were courtesans, conquistadors-killers, and kings-fools; the red-bearded giant Barbarossa never gave a thought to knowledge or fantasy or love of the unknown; and perhaps, as he was drowning in the river, he didn't remember what he would have had he obeyed the laws of his imaginary life, which we were to create for him many hundreds of years after his death. When I thought about this everything appeared unreal and diffused, like shadows wavering in smoke.

And once again I would turn from such strained but arbitrary perceptions to what I saw around me and to a closer knowledge of the people who surrounded me; this was all the more important since I already felt the approaching necessity of leaving them and, perhaps, never seeing them again. But when I fixed my attention upon them, I would notice their insufficiencies and laughable sides more often than anything else, and wouldn't notice their merits—partly because of my inability to distinguish one person from another and partly because I felt very critical towards them but was nearly incapable of interpreting or understanding them. This latter art developed considerably later, and even then it was often feigned, although at times it could be sincere and pure-hearted. I took pleasure in loving certain people without becoming particularly close to them, because there remained in them something which had not been expressed. And while I knew that this unexpressed thing was no doubt something simple and common, I would nonetheless involuntarily create illusions for myself which could not have arisen if everything had been expressed. Of all such people I loved most Boris Belov, an engineer who had just finished the technological institute. He was known for never being serious, and when cadet Volodya, who had a wonderful voice (he was on leave from some partisan detachment or other, and in describing him to someone Belov said, "Vladimir, singer and partisan"), sang the romance "Quietude" in the Voronin's boarding house, and had gotten to the part where the moon emerges from behind a linden tree, behind his back Belov, waving his hands and puffing like a man who has fallen in the water, depicted a floating moon. Just as Volodya finished singing Belov said:

"I'd pay quite a sum for irrefutable proof that the moon actually swims and that linden trees are made of lace," and the artist Severny, who was also standing there, remarked with a sorrowful smile:

"You always joke . . .": Since he himself had no sense of humor and never joked, he didn't like jokers. He was always sad. "An invincible man," Belov said about him, "and a champion of melancholy." But what was most astonishing about him was that no man on earth possessed such an unbelievable appetite.

"Severny, why are you always so sad?" a young lady once asked him. And Severny, with a bitter smile and absent-mindedly looking in front of him answered:

"It's hard to say. . ." but Belov interrupted the splendid pause that followed this sentence by declaring, "To whom might I recount my sorrow?" For all this, Belov turned out to be more than just a joker. Once, when I had come to see him unannounced, I heard someone playing a serenade by Tozelli on the violin as I neared the house, and I saw that the person playing was Belov himself.

"What? You play the violin?" I said in amazement. He said simply, neither joking nor laughing but in a normal tone:

"There is nothing in the world better than music."

And thereupon he added:

"And it's a pity not to possess any talents."

Then he suddenly came to himself and, repeating the sentence "there's nothing better than music," although already in his other, more usual tone he said, "Except, perhaps, melon?" and he made a brooding face. But I already knew what he had thought necessary to hide. This man who laughed at everything feared mockery more than anything else, and after this incident Belov began to behave more reservedly around me than he had before.

The artist Severny was a very narrow-minded person. He was usually silent, but made up for it by invariably talking nonsense once he began to speak. He was extremely pleased with his own paintings, his looks and his success with women.

"You know," he would say, "I'm not a bad-looking guy. One day I was coming out of the theater and running nervously after me was a famous actress and she said, 'Who are you? What's your name? Listen, I'll go wait for you at your house. . .' What could I do? I smiled regretfully (he said it just like that, "I smiled regretfully") and answered, 'My dear, I don't like actresses.' She bit her lip until it bled, tapped her fan on her chin and, turning sharply around, walked away. I shrugged my shoulders." "I must write this down," said Belov. "So you say she bit her lip and turned around sharply, despite the blow of the fan, which she was holding in front of her chin? And you smiled regretfully?" Severny didn't answer, and began to walk about his studio. This studio was, by the way, a small, tidy room with symmetrically hung paintings. Belov, who went there once, was struck by a drawing of a bird's head holding some morsel in its mouth which looked like a fragment of iron. Beneath the painting were the words, "Study of a Swan." Belov asked mistrustfully "Is this an *étude*?"

"It is," said Severny gruffly.

"And what's an *étude*?"

"Well you see . . ." answered Severny after thinking a moment, "it's a French word." He looked around and his glance came to rest on Smirnov, his closest friend and admirer. With a nod of his head Smirnov confirmed Severny's words.

Smirnov understood nothing about painting, just as he understood nothing that went beyond the limits of his extremely modest knowledge. He studied in the same gymnasium as myself, but was three grades ahead, and at the time of his friendship with Severny he was a student at the local university. He always carried revolutionary brochures, proclamations and a ready supply of ideas on cooperation and collectivism; but he knew these issues only through popularized books, was weak in the history of socialism, and knew nothing about Saint-Simon's sectarianism, Owen's theory of bankruptcy, or the crazy bookkeeper who waited all his life for the great eccentric who would give him a million so that, with the help of this money, he could build happiness in France and then across the entire globe. I asked Smirnov, "Aren't you tired of these brochures?"

"They will help us free the people." I didn't object; but Belov broke into the conversation, "You're absolutely certain that the people wouldn't manage without you?" he asked.

"If everyone reasons like that, we will never become a conscious nation," Smirnov answered.

"Look," Belov said, turning to me, "what the brochures have done to this nice man. Never has there existed anywhere a conscious nation. Why, with the help of illiterate pamphlets, will all of us suddenly become conscious, and Smirnov read to us about the evolutionary theory of value, and Marfa, our cook, a woman of remarkable virtues, read to us about the time of the early Renaissance? Smirnov, give these brochures to Severny. Tell him they're *études*." But here it turned out that Severny had long been a communist and party member. Belov was delighted to hear this, shook Severny's hand and said, "Well, my dear fellow, I congratulate you. And I thought he only drew *études*."

Smirnov, speaking always in that strange and pompous language of agitprop remarked, "Your empty irony, Belov, could alienate valuable workers from our ranks."

"This isn't a human being," said Belov, turning to me and Severny. "No, this is a newspaper. And not even a newspaper, but a feature article. You're a feature article, do you understand?"

"I may understand more than you think."

"What verbs!" Belov uttered derisively. "To understand, to think. The ideology of the cooperative would never accept such things."

But Belov's mockery had no effect on either Severny or Smirnov since, apart from being stupid, they were under the sway of the fashion governing the political conversations and socio-economic debates of the times. This fashion left me indifferent. I was interested only in those abstract ideas which I could relate to and which would have a cherished and important meaning for me; I could sit for hours pouring over a book by Boehme but was unable to read a single work on cooperation. And while I found discussions of political issues—Russia and the Revolution—strange, I found their sense, or rather their movements, even stranger. I thought about them as I did everything else, most often at night; the lamp above my table was lit, outside the window it was cold and dark; and I lived as if I were on a distant island; right there, beyond the window and beyond the wall, ghosts crowded together, coming into the room as soon as I thought about them. The air was cold in Russia then, snow was deep, houses appeared black, music played and everything flowed by in front of me. And everything lacked verisimilitude, slowly passed by and then would stop, only suddenly to begin moving once again; one image ran into another as though the wind were blowing on the flames of a candle and trembling shadows began to leap along the wall, called there suddenly by God knows what power, flying, God knows why, like the black, silent visions in my dreams. And when my eyes became tired I would shut them, and it was as if a door had slammed shut in front of me; then an underground noise from the darkness and the depths rose up, which I listened to without seeing, without understanding its sense, attempting to grasp it and to remember it. I heard in it both the rustle of the sand and the rumble of the trembling earth, the whining diving sound of some speeding flight and the motifs of the accordions and a street organ; and finally the voice of a lame soldier would reach me:

The Moscow fire burned and roared . . .

and then I would open my eyes again and see the smoke and the red flames lighting the cold winter streets. It was unbelievably cold at the time: In school—I was in the sixth grade—we sat without taking our coats off and the teachers walked around in their fur coats. They were very rarely paid a salary, and in spite of this they always came to class. There were several subjects which had no one to teach them, several hours' worth, and we would take advantage of this freedom to sing convict songs to the whole class which we had learned from Perenko, a tall boy of about eighteen who lived in the troubled outskirts of town and was growing up among future thieves and possibly even killers. He had a Finnish dagger, always spoke with crude words, clicking his tongue in some special way and spitting through his teeth. He was a wonderful comrade and a bad student—not because he lacked ability, but rather because his parents were simple people, and no one in his family could help him with his studies. In a small apartment adjacent to the shop which his father ran, no one knew the Hundred Years' War, nor the War of Red and White Roses, and all of these names and foreign words and complex events of modern history, the laws of heat, and passages from the French and German classics, all of this was so alien to Perenko that he could neither understand nor remember any of it; nor, finally, could he feel that it had the least meaning which could, at least to some degree, have been useful to him. Perenko could have become interested in these things had his spiritual needs not found another outlet. But, like the majority of people of this type, he was extremely sentimental, and he sang his labor songs practically with tears in his eyes. For him these songs replaced the mental excitement which books, theater and music aroused, and his need of this stimulation was perhaps stronger than it was for his more educated peers. Most of the teachers didn't know this and thought Perenko was a simple hooligan; only the Russian teacher treated him at all seriously and paid attention to him, and never laughed at his ignorance, for which Perenko loved him dearly and singled him out.

This teacher seemed like a strange man to us. This was because he didn't talk about things in his lessons which we were used to, things I had learned over and over again for five years, until I changed schools—the one where Vasily Nikolaevich taught; they called him Vasily Nikolaevich. "I gave you the name Lev Tolstoy," he said. "And you know, he had a special connotation among the people. For example, my mother, an altogether simple woman, a seamstress, once wanted to go to Tolstoy after my father's death to consult him on what she should do; her situation was bad and she was very poor. She wanted to go to Tolstoy because she thought he was the last saint and wise man left on earth. We have a different point of view, but my mother was simpler than we are and would certainly not have understood the psychology of Anna Karenina or Prince Andrei, and especially not that of Princess Helene Bezukhov; her ideas were uncomplicated, but stronger and more sincere for it; and this, gentleman, is a great happiness." Then he would go on to talk about Trediakovsky, would explain the difference between syllabic and tonic versification and would say, by way of conclusion:

"Trediakovsky was an unfortunate man who lived in a cruel era. His position was humiliating. Imagine, given the rudeness of court manners in those days, having to play a role that was half buffoon and half poet. Derzhavin was much happier than he."

Vasily Nikolaevich himself resembled a heretical holy man, with his grey beard and simple iron glasses; he spoke quickly, in that northern Russian tongue which sounds so strange in the Ukraine. He dressed in a very slovenly and indigent manner; a stranger seeing him on the street would never suspect that this old man was a wonderful and educated pedagogue. There was something of the zealot about him. I remembered his sullen, grey eyebrows and the reddened eyes that peered through his glasses, remembered his sincerity, courage and simplicity: He concealed neither his convictions, which might have seemed too far to the left under the Hetman or too far to the right under the Bolsheviks, nor that his mother was a seamstress—something one would rarely confess. At the time we had been studying the priest Avvakum, and Vasily Nikolaevich would read us long passages:

". . . And just as the day of Sabbath dawned, they put me in a tumbler and stretched my arms apart, and drove from the Patriarch's court to the monastery of Andronicus, and there they put chains on me and threw me into a black dungeon, dug into the earth, and I lay there for three days with nothing to eat or drink; sitting in the darkness I bowed down to the earth, knowing not which way was east or west. No one came to me but mice and black beetles, and the chirp of crickets, and fleas in abundance. And by the third day I was ravenous—that is to say, I wanted to eat—and after vespers someone came and stood before me, I knew not whether angel or man, and to this day still do not know. I only know that there in the darkness he said a prayer and, taking me by the shoulder, led me with my chain to a bench and sat me down on it and put a spoon in my hands and gave me a morsel of bread and some cabbage soup to eat—Oh, but it tasted good!—and he said to me: 'Enough, that will do to fortify you.' And then he was gone . . . They removed my chain and, with a monk guarding me, dragged me to the church. In the church they pulled at my hair, poked my ribs and tugged at my chain and spat in my eyes. May God forgive them in this life and the next: It was not they themselves who did this to me, but Satan, the Evil One."

And likewise at another time another officer turned on me like a wild beast. Breaking into my house, he beat me and gnawed at the fingers of my hand with his teeth, like a dog; and when his gizzard had filled with blood he loosened his teeth from my hand and, tossing me aside, went to his house. But I, thanking the Lord, wrapped my hand in a cloth and started out for vespers; and on the way he fell upon me again, this time with two small pistols and from right next to me fired from one of them and, by the will of God, the powder exploded in the pan and the pistol misfired. He flung himself on the ground and fired again from the other pistol, and God willed the same thing to happen, and this pistol also misfired. Praying assiduously to the dear Lord, with one hand I made the sign of the cross over him and bowed deeply before him; at this he began to growl at me, but I said to him,

'Into thy orifices, Ivan Rodionovich, let blessing enter!' upon which he grew even wilder with rage: he wanted me to speak faster, he was so annoyed, but I speak slowly, according to the custom. Next he took me from my yard, beat me, took all my possessions and left me there on the road without a penny."

He read extremely well; my friend Shchur, one of the most talented and intelligent people whom I had ever met, said to me, "You know, Vasily Nikolaevich himself resembles Archpriest Avvakum; it's people like them who burned at the stake."

"Who here knows the legend of the dancer Our Mother of God?" Vasily Nikolaevich once asked. Only one boy in the class knew this legend. This was a Jewish boy with a tender child's face by the name of Rosenberg. He was so small that, by his appearance, you would think he was eleven or twelve, while in fact he was already sixteen. In the morning girls from the eighth grade would shout at him when they saw him on the street, "Little boy, little boy, run faster—you're late!" and Rosenberg would be humiliated to tears. He was brighter and more mature for his age than one would have expected: He read and remembered a great deal, and often knew strange things which he had read in some big almanac or other, and these things stuck in his memory: the means of fertilization in Mexico, the religious superstitions of the Polynesians and anecdotes pertaining to the time of the founding of the British parliament. And this Rosenberg knew the legend of the dancer Our Mother of God. "Why," he said, asking for an explanation from Vasily Nikolaevich, "how could one *not* know it?" But nonetheless the majority of the students in the class had never heard it before, and Vasily Nikolaevich told it to us: Everyone listened attentively, and Perenko, looking straight at his Finnish dagger, remained seated and, eyes fixed on the white metal, was deep in thought. Two days later, Vasily Nikolaevich asked us to read the beginning of the latest biography of Tolstoy, where there was a mention of the Ant Brothers: and even Rosenberg knew nothing about the Ant Brothers. That same day I insulted the new priest, who had just arrived at the school wearing a silk cassock and lacquered boots. He came into class for the first time, crossed himself, rather coquettishly I thought, looked around at the students and said,

"Gentlemen, it seems that nowadays the Scriptures and the history of the church are not in fashion." He shook his head, pursed his lips and cackled ironically a few times. "Perhaps there are atheists among you who do not wish to be present at my lessons. If there are," he smiled mockingly and wrung his hands, "let them stand up and leave the class." As he said the words, "leave the class" he became serious and severe, as if emphasizing the fact that he had finished with mocking the ignorant atheists and that there was no question of anyone wanting to leave the class. This man was saturated with pride and never let slip an occasion to remind us that religion was now persecuted and that sometimes it required exceptional courage on the part of priests, as it had at the beginning of Christianity, and he would cite sacred texts to the class, continually, moreover, misquoting them and forcing Saint John to utter words belonging to Thomas Aquinas. But I believe that this was of little importance to him. He was not defending religious dogma, an area in which he was weak, but something else. And this something else expressed itself by his becoming used to the position of one "persecuted" and, little by little, growing so accustomed to it that, had religion become respected once more, there would have been absolutely nothing for him to do and it would probably all have become very tiresome and boring for him.

I got up and left the classroom. He followed me with his eyes and said, "Do you remember the place in the liturgy, 'Devils, be gone!'"

After a week Vasily Nikolaevich asked me, "You, Sosedov, do you believe in God?"

"No, and you, Vasily Nikolaevich?"

"I'm a very religious person. He who is able to believe until the very end is truly happy."

In general, the words he used most often were "happy" and "unhappy." He was one of those irreconcilable Russians who see the meaning of life in the search for truth even if they become convinced that truth, in the sense in which they understand it, does not and cannot exist. For him the teaching of Russian always involved remarks on things which often had no immediate relation to the subject at hand, such as current events, religion and history; and through it all he displayed an astonishing erudition. It would suddenly come out that he had lived abroad, had spent many years in Switzerland, England and France, knew foreign languages quite well and paid attention to everything that he had seen. He was always searching for his truth wherever he was. Later I often thought to myself, "Would he find it? Would he have sufficient courage to lie to himself and would he die happy?" And it seemed to me that even if he thought that he had found his truth, he most certainly would hasten to renounce it, only to begin searching all over again; perhaps his truth didn't include the naive idea that it is possible to find that which we never possessed; and certainly it did not consist in the dream of peace and quiet, since this intellectual inactivity to which he would have been condemned would have been a shame and torment for him. Vasily Nikolaevich was one of three teachers whom I liked in all the time I spent at various institutions. All the rest were narrow-minded people concerned only with their careers and who saw teaching as mere employment. The worst of all—the dullest and most ignorant pedagogues—were the clergymen. Only my first teacher of law, an academician and philosopher, seemed to me a rather remarkable man, even though a fanatic. He was not a pedant; in the fifth grade when I would ask him at length about the atheistic meaning of "The Grand Inquisitor" and about *The Life of Jesus* by Renan—at the time I was reading *The Brothers Karamazov* and Renan, but hadn't studied the course and knew neither the catechism, or the history of the church—he didn't once take me to task, and only after the last quarter did he quietly say, waving me over to himself with a finger,

"Do you think, Kolya," he called us all by the familiar form as he had been our teacher since the first grade, "that I have no idea just how much of the catechism you know? Dear boy, I know everything. But I'll give you an 'A' anyway because you're at least somewhat interested in religion. Now you can go." When he gave his sermons tears would come to his eyes; but apparently he did not believe in God. He reminded me of the Grand Inquisitor in miniature: He was invincible in dialectical questions and in general would have been a better Catholic than an Orthodox believer. He had a wonderful voice, strong and intelligent. I repeatedly noticed that a person's voice, just like his face, can be intelligent or stupid, talented or dull, noble or base. He was killed several years later during the Civil War somewhere in the south, and the news of his death was that much more painful to me since in general I didn't like clergymen and therefore had acted badly towards this man who was no longer among the living.

I didn't know, actually, why I harbored an aversion to people of holy orders. Perhaps it was my conviction that they stood on a lower social level than the rest—they and policemen, that is. You could not shake their hand, could not invite them to dine with you, and I remembered the long figure of the police officer who used to come to receive his monthly payoff, Lord knows for what, patiently waiting in the anteroom while the maid brought him money, after which he would give a sprightly cough and leave, clacking the huge spurs of his lacquered boots with their extraordinarily short tops, the kind only policemen and, for some reason, regents of the church choir, wore. Once I even saw how clergymen could be bribed. I was in the third grade when I became ill for two weeks before Easter and didn't fast in the school church, and Father John told me that I would have to bring a certificate of fasting to school in the fall or I would be left back a year. That summer I went, as I almost always did, to Kislovodsk. My uncle Vitaly was a skeptic and romantic who remained a dragoon captain all his life, the result of challenging the commander of his regiment to a duel—and in response to the latter's refusal to fight slapped him in the face at an officers' meeting and proceeded to spend five years in prison, from which he left a very changed man and where he acquired a surprising and, for an officer, unusual erudition in questions of art, philosophy and social science; afterwards he continued to be a part of that regiment but never advanced in rank—my uncle Vitaly said to me:

"Kolya, take ten rubles and go to that long-maned idiot. Ask him for a certificate of fasting. There's no point in going to church and idling about. Simply give him the money and take the certificate from him." Uncle Vitaly always cursed everybody and was dissatisfied with everything, although in his personal manner and in his relations with people he was usually kind and tolerant, and when my aunt wanted to punish her eight-year-old son he would defend him by saying, "You leave him in peace. He doesn't understand what he's done. Don't forget that this boy is strikingly stupid and he's not about to get any smarter by your flogging him. Besides, one generally should not beat children, and only an ignorant woman like yourself doesn't know this." Uncle began almost every one of his conversations with the words, "Those idiots . . ."

"The clergyman won't give me a certificate so easily," I said. "Really, I must fast first."

"That's a lot of nonsense. Pay him ten rubles and nothing more. Do as I tell you."

I went to the priest. He lived in a small apartment with two yellow armchairs and portraits of eminent clergymen on the walls. In response to my question about the certificate he said, "My son," his address jarred me, "come to church. First confess, then take communion, then after a week you will be able to receive a certificate."

"Can't I get it now?"

"No."

"I would have liked one now, Father."

"You can't have one now," said the priest, growing angry at my slow-wittedness. At that moment I took out the ten rubles and placed them on the table, and I did not look at the priest because I was ashamed. He took the money, stuffed it in his pocket, having thrown back the flap of his cassock and displaying narrow, black trousers with footstraps beneath it, and called out, "Father Deacon!" From the neighboring room the deacon appeared chewing on something; his face was covered with sweat from the unusual heat and, as he was very fat, the sweat literally streamed from him. Bright drops hung from his eyebrows. "Give the young man his certificate of fasting." The deacon nodded his head and immediately wrote out a certificate for me in rather pretty, special square handwriting.

"What did I tell you," muttered Uncle. "Brother, I know them . . ."

My aunt remarked to him, "You shouldn't say such things to the boy," and he answered, "This boy, like any other boy, understands no less than you do. Mother, I know this well. The day you begin to teach me something is the day I hang myself." In the evenings Vitaly sat on the terrace of the house, lost in thought. "Why do you sit for so long on the terrace?" I would ask. "I lose myself in thought," Vitaly answered, and would say the words as if he actually were lost in thought, as if in water or in a bath. Once in a while he would talk with me:

"What grade are you in?"

"In the fourth."

"What are you studying now?"

"Various subjects."

"They're teaching you nothing but nonsense. What do you know about Peter the Great and Catherine? Well, tell me."

I would tell him. After I finished speaking I waited for him to say, "Those idiots. . ."

And sure enough he would say:

"Those idiots are teaching you falsehoods."

"Why falsehoods?" I asked.

"Because they're idiots," Vitaly said with conviction. "They think it's a good thing if you have the false impression that Russian history has been a steady stream of good and intelligent monarchs. In fact what you're learning is a kind of sugar-coated mythology with which they have replaced historical fact, and as a result you'll turn out to be a fool. But you'll turn out to be a fool anyway, even if you know true history."

"For sure?"

"For sure. Everyone does."

"And you, for example?"

"You're insolent," he said perfectly calmly. "One shouldn't ask such questions of one's elders. But if you want to know I, too, take my place among fools, although I'd like things to be otherwise."

"But what can be done?"

"Be a scoundrel," he said sharply and turned away.

He had an unfortunate marriage, lived cut off from nearly all of his family and knew that his wife, a very beautiful woman from Moscow, was unfaithful to him; he was much older than she. I went to Kislovodsk every summer and would always find Vitaly there, until the movements of the various Bolshevik and anti-Bolshevik battles that were taking place on the Don and in Kuban forced me out of the Caucasus. Only a year before my departure from Russia, while the Civil War was going on, I went there again and once again saw the figure of Vitaly hunched over in an armchair on the terrace of our dacha. He had grown old since I had last seen him, his hair had turned grey and his face had become even more gloomy than before. "I met Alexandra Pavlovna in the park (this was his wife)," I said to him in greeting. "She looks lovely." Vitaly looked at me sullenly.

"Do you remember Pushkin's epigrams?"

"Yes."

He recited:

There is no one like you on earth
All the world grows hard, and I with it,
Another may age with the passage of time
But you, with each year, grow younger.

"You look discontent, Vitaly."

"What's to be done? Brother, I'm an old pessimist. They tell me you want to join the army?"

"Yes."

"You're doing a stupid thing."

"Why?"

I thought he would say, "Those idiots," but he didn't. He only lowered his head and uttered, "Because in war the volunteers lose."

The idea of whether the volunteers won or lost at war didn't much interest me. I wanted to know what war was, that same desire I always had for the new and the unknown. I joined the White Army because I was on its territory, because it was expected of me; and if in those days the Reds had occupied Kislovodsk, I probably would have joined the Red Army. But I was surprised that Vitaly, an old officer, reacted to this with such disapproval. I did not then fully understand that Vitaly was too intelligent for this and did not attach as much importance to his rank as one usually does. But I nonetheless asked him why he thought that way. Looking at me with indifference he said that they, that is, those who commanded the anti-governmental troops, didn't know the laws of social relations. "Out there," he said, growing animated "out there is all of starving northern Russia. That is where the *muzhiks* are. Did you know that Russia was a country made up of peasants, or didn't they teach you that in your history class?"

"I know," I answered.

Then Vitaly continued: "Russia," he said, "is entering the zone of the peasant stage of history, the strength of the *muzhik*, and the *muzhik* serves in the Red Army. The Whites," according to Vitaly's contemptuous observation, "don't even possess that romanticism of war which could seem attractive; the White

Army is the army of the middle class and the semi-intelligentsia. It's full of madmen, cocaine addicts, cavalry officers mincing like coquettes," Vitaly said sharply. "Failed careerists and sergeant majors can be found in the ranks of the generals."

"You always curse everything," I remarked. "Alexandra Pavlovna says that it's your *profession de foi.*"

"Alexandra Pavlovna, Alexandra Pavlovna," said Vitaly with unexpected exasperation. "*Profession de foi*—what nonsense. I've been hearing this senseless objection 'you curse everything' for twenty years now, and from all sides. Do I have something in mind or don't I? I give you an account of the reasons for the inevitability of a certain outcome to the war and you tell me 'you curse everything.' What are you, a man or Aunt Zhenya? I reproached Alexandra Pavlovna for always reading cheap trash and she, too, told me I was just cursing everything as usual. No, not everything. Literature, thank God, I know and love better than my wife does. If I curse something it's because I have a reason to. You understand," said Vitaly lifting his head, "that out of everything that is done in any region, whether reforms, the reorganization of the army or attempts to introduce new methods into education, painting or literature, nine out of ten attempts don't work. This is always the case; why am I guilty if Aunt Zhenya doesn't understand this?" He was silent for a moment and then asked abrubtly,

"How old are you?"

"I'll be sixteen in two months."

"And the devil leads you to go to war?"

"Yes."

"But why, actually, are you going to war?" Vitaly suddenly uttered in surprise. I didn't know how to answer him, faltered and finally said without conviction, "I think it's nonetheless my duty."

"I thought you were more intelligent than that," Vitaly said disappointedly. "If your father were alive he would not be pleased to hear your words."

"Why?"

"Listen, my dear boy," said Vitaly with unexpected gentleness. "Try to understand. Two sides are fighting, the Reds and the Whites. The Whites are attempting to return Russia to that historical state which it has just left. The Reds are leading it into a chaos which it has not known since the time of Tsar Alexei Mikhailovich."

"The end of the Time of Troubles," I muttered.

"Yes, the end of the Time of Troubles. I see school taught you something," and Vitaly set forth to give me his view on the events of those times. He said that social categories—these words struck me since I could never forget that Vitaly was an officer of the dragoon regiment—were like phenomena subordinated to the laws of a kind of non-material biology, and that such a concept was, if not always infallible, often applicable to different social events. "These," said Vitaly, "are born, grow, and die, and they don't even really die but die off, like coral. Do you remember how coral islands form?"

"Yes," I said. "I remember how they rise up and I also remember their red curves surrounded by the white spume of the sea. It's quite beautiful. I saw a drawing of them in one of my father's books."

"The very same process occurs in history," continued Vitaly. "One thing dies off, another is conceived. So, to put it crudely, the Whites are like dying coral, on the corpses of which new formations are growing. The Reds—they are what is growing."

"Good, let's admit that this is so," I said. Vitaly's eyes once again took on their usual mocking expression. "But doesn't it seem to you that truth is on the side of the Whites?"

"Truth? What kind of truth? In the sense that they are right in attempting to seize power?"

"Perhaps," I said, even though I thought otherwise.

"Yes. Of course, but the Reds are also right and then so are the Greens, and if there were Oranges and Violets, then they would also would be right."

"And besides, the front is already at Orel, and the forces of Kolchak are coming to the Volga."

"That doesn't mean anything. If you're still alive after all this carnage has ceased, you shall read in specialized books the detailed accounts of the heroic defeat of the Whites and the infamous accidental victory of the Reds—that is, if the book is written by scholars sympathetic to the Whites—and about the heroic victory of the workers' army over the mercenary bourgeoisie, if the author is on the side of the Reds."

I answered that I was nonetheless going to fight on the side of the Whites, since they were losing.

"That's schoolboy sentimentalism," Vitaly said tolerantly. "All right, I'll tell you what I think. Not about everything that can be derived from an analysis of the forces directing current events, but my own convictions. Don't forget that I'm an officer and a conservative in the basic sense of this word and, above all else, a man with an almost feudal notion of honor and justice."

"What do you think?"

He took a deep breath and said:

"Truth is on the side of the Reds."

In the evening he invited me to go with him to the park. We walked along the red alleyways, along the bright, small stream and the miniature grottos, under the tall, venerable trees. It grew dark, the stream sobbed and babbled; and for me this quiet noise is now mingled with the memory of our leisurely walk on the sand with the lights from the restaurant visible from far off, and with the fact that whenever I lowered my head I noticed my white summer pants and Vitaly's tall boots. Vitaly was more talkative than usual, and I did not hear the customary irony in his voice. He said seriously and simply, as we went deeper into the park, "So then, you're going, Nikolai. Do you hear the babbling of the stream?" he suddenly interrupted himself. I listened, and through the even noise my hearing detected several babblings, simultaneous and yet distinct.

"It's an incomprehensible thing," said Vitaly. "Why does this noise disturb me so? For many years now, each time I hear it I always have the impression that I have never heard it before. But there was something else I wanted to say."

"I'm listening."

"I most surely will never see you again," he said. "Either you'll be killed or you'll wind up on the other end of the earth or, finally, having been unable to wait for your return, I will die my own death. This is equally possible."

"Why are you so gloomy?" I asked. I could never imagine events a long time in advance. I was scarcely able to grasp what was happening to me right then and there, and that was why all suppositions about what could happen always struck me as nonsensical. Vitaly told me that he had been the same in his youth; but five years of solitary confinement had nourished his fantasy exclusively with ideas about the future, and developed this fantasy to unusual proportions. Reviewing any event which, according to him, would soon happen, Vitaly immediately saw its many sides, and it was as if his refined imagination had a premonition of this elusive psychological membrane and the membrane of external events, beneath which this event could take place. Besides which, his knowledge of people and the reasons which compelled them to act in such or another manner was incomparably richer than the common life experience natural for a man of his age; this gave him, at first glance, an almost incomprehensible ability for guessing, something which I found only among my very rare and somehow always accidental acquaintances. Vitaly almost never put this skill to use, however, because he was disdainfully indifferent to the fate of even his close relatives. And his kindness and tolerance could be explained, as I saw it, by this almost always unvarying and indifferent relation to everyone.

"I loved your father very much," Vitaly said without answering my question, "even though he always chided me for being an officer and cavalier. But maybe he was right. And I love you," he continued, "and so, before you leave, I want to tell you one thing. Keep this in mind."

I didn't know what Vitaly wanted to say to me: In my relationship with him there was somehow no room for the idea that he could take an interest in me and advise me on anything. He always preferred to scold me for my lack of understanding of something, or for my love of discussions on abstract subjects about which, in his words, I didn't understand a thing; once he laughed until he nearly cried when I told him that I had read

Stirner and Kropotkin, and another time he shook his head grievously when he learned of my passion for the works of Victor Hugo; he spoke scornfully of this man who, as he put it, had the understanding of a fireman, the spirit of a sentimental fool, and the pomposity of a Russian telegraph operator.

"Listen to me," Vitaly meanwhile said to me. "In the near future you will be witnessing many atrocities. You will see people killed, hung, shot. None of this is new, important, or very interesting, but here is what I advise you: Don't ever become a man of conviction. Don't reason or draw conclusions, but try to be as simple as possible. And remember that the greatest happiness on earth is to think that you've understood something about the life surrounding you. But you won't understand. It will only seem to you that you understand and when, after some time, you look back on it you will see that you had not truly understood. And after another year or two has passed you will be convinced that you were mistaken the second time as well. And so it will go without end. And nonetheless this is the most important and the most interesting thing in life."

"Very well," I said, "but what sense is there to these continual mistakes?"

"Sense?" said Vitaly in surprise. "There is no sense at all. No, and none is necessary either."

"It can't be. There is a law of expediency."

"No, my dear boy. Meaning is a fiction and so is expediency. Look, if you take several phenomena and begin to analyze them, you will see that there are certain forces guiding their movements; but an understanding of their sense won't influence either these forces or these movements. Take any historical fact resulting from lengthy politics and preparations which has a fully determined outcome. You will see that from the point of view of achieving this and only this goal, such an act makes no sense, because at the same time as it is occurring and, it would seem, for the very same reasons, other entirely unforeseen events are occurring, and everything changes completely."

He looked at me; we went between two rows of trees and it was so dark that I could barely see his face.

"The word 'sense'," continued Vitaly, "would cease to be a fiction only if we were to possess exact knowledge of the fact that when we will act in a certain way, there will always be a certain result and not others. But seeing as this is often unpredictable, even in the primitive mechanical sciences with specific goals in mind and under equally specific conditions, then how do you expect it to be a certainty in the realm of social relations, the nature of which we do not understand, or in the realm of psychology, whose laws we are practically ignorant of? There is no sense, my dear Kolya."

"But isn't there a meaning to life?"

Vitaly suddenly stopped short, as if something had detained him. It was completely dark out. Through the leaves of the trees the sky was practically invisible. The animated park and the town remained far below; on the left, the Romanovsky mountain, covered with firs, looked blue. It seemed blue to me even though then, in the dark, the eye must have seen it as black. But I was used to seeing it in the daytime when it actually did look blue, and in the evening I would use my sight only in order to better remember the contours of the mountain, and its blue color was already there in my imagination in spite of the laws of color and distance. The air was very pure and fresh; once again, as always in the quiet, a distinct, drawn out and distant sound came to me from afar, dying out up above.

"The meaning of life?" Vitaly repeated sadly, and I heard tears in his voice and I didn't believe what I was hearing; I always thought that tears were unknown to this courageous and indifferent man.

"I had a comrade who also asked me about the meaning of life," said Vitaly, "before he shot himself. He was my very close friend, a great comrade," he said, repeating the word comrade over and over, as if finding some kind of elusive consolation in the fact that, many years later, this word sounded just as it had before and resounded in the still air of the empty park. "He was a student at the time and I was a cadet. He always asked me, 'Why do we need such a horrid, nonsensical existence, this awareness that if I die an old man and, while dying, am repulsive to everyone, that this is somehow a good thing—what good is that? Why live to that point? There's no escape from death, Vitaly, do you understand? There is no salvation!' 'None!' Vitaly had cried. 'Why,' he continued, 'become an engineer or a lawyer or a writer or an officer, why live through such degradation and shame, such baseness and cowardice?' I would then tell him that one still could live outside of such questions, live, eat steak, kiss one's mistress, bemoan the fickleness of women, and be happy. And let God steer you from asking yourself why you're doing all of it. But he didn't believe me. He shot himself. And now you ask me the meaning of life. I can't answer you. I don't know."

That day we returned home very late; when the sluggish maid brought us tea out on the terrace, Vitaly looked at the glass, lifted it up and gazed through the fluid to the electric lamp, and he laughed for a long time without uttering a word. Then he muttered derisively, "the meaning of life," and suddenly frowned, and his eyes grew dark and he left to go to bed, without wishing me goodnight.

When, some time later, I was leaving Kislovodsk for the Ukraine, where I would join the army, Vitaly said goodbye to me calmly and coldly, and in his eyes there was once again that eternally indifferent expression, ready at a moment's notice to turn into mockery. I was sorry to leave him because I loved him dearly, and because those around him were afraid of him and did not particularly like him. "A heart of stone," his wife said of him. "A cruel man," my aunt said. "He holds nothing sacred," echoed his daughter-in-law. Not one of them knew the real Vitaly. Later on, as I ruminated about his dismal end and unfortunate life I grieved that a man of such huge talents and with such a lively, quick mind had gone to waste like that. And not one of the people close to him felt sorry for him. As I left, I knew that we would probably never meet again. I wanted to embrace Vitaly and say goodbye to him like someone who was close to me and not simply an acquaintance who had come to the station, but Vitaly conducted himself quite officially; and when, with a flick of his finger, he knocked a bit of fluff from his sleeve, I understood through this one gesture that to say goodbye as I had wanted would have been absurd and *ridicule*. He shook my hand: I left. It was late autumn, and in the cold air I could feel the sorrow and the regret characteristic of every departure. I was never able to accustom myself to this feeling; for me, every departure marked the beginning of a new existence and consequently, the necessity of living once again by groping, of finding once more among the people and things surrounding me, a more or less intimate environment in which to recapture my former tranquility, so needed to make space for those inner oscillations and shocks with which I was so greatly preoccupied. I was also sorry to be leaving the cities where I had lived and the people I had met, because these cities and people would not repeat themselves in my life; their real, simple immobility and the determinedness of their fixed images were like no other countries, cities or people living in my imagination and which I called into existence and motion. I had the power to destroy and create over some things, and over others my only power was my memory, my feeble knowledge. And this knowledge was insufficient even for guessing that gift which Vitaly possessed. I saw his figure standing on the platform for some time; but Kislovodsk had already begun to disappear and the sounds coming from the station were drowned out by the iron roar of the train; and when I came to that city where I had studied and lived during the winter, I saw that snow was falling, melting into the light of the lanterns. Smartly dressed cabbies cried out along the streets, tramways thundered, and the lit windows of the houses were passing by me, passing behind the wide, quilted back of the cabby who was throwing his elbows up as he held the reins in disorderly and bustling movements, like the jerking arms and legs of a wooden toy clown. I lived in this city for a week before my dispatch to the front; I passed the time by going to the theater and to cabarets, and to crowded restaurants with Rumanian orchestras. The day before I had to leave I met Shchur, a high-school comrade; he was very surprised to see me in uniform.

"You're not joining the volunteers, are you?"

When I answered that I was, he looked at me with still greater astonishment.

"What are you doing? Have you gone crazy? Stay here. The volunteers are retreating, and in two weeks our people will be in the city."

"No, I've already decided to go."

"What a queer fish you are. You'll regret it later."

"Well, I'm going anyway."

He firmly shook my hand. "I hope you won't be disappointed."

"Thanks, I don't think I will be."

"Do you believe the volunteers will win?"

"Not at all, that's why I won't be disappointed." In the evening I said goodbye to Mother. My leaving was a blow to her. She asked me to stay; I needed all the cruelty of my sixteen years to leave Mother alone and go off to war, without conviction, without enthusiasm, exclusively out of a desire finally to see and understand in war such things as might regenerate me.

"Fate took my husband and daughters from me," Mother told me. "Only you are left, and now you're leaving."

I didn't respond.

"Your father," Mother continued, "would have been very upset to learn that Nikolai was joining the army of those whom he had always despised."

"Uncle Vitaly told me the same thing," I answered. "Don't worry, Mother, the war will be over soon and I'll be home again."

"And if it's your corpse they bring me?"

"No, I know they won't kill me." She stood at the door in the front hall and silently looked at me, slowly shutting and opening her eyes like someone who is just coming to their senses after having fainted. I picked up my suitcase: One of its clasps got caught on the hem of my coat and, seeing that I could not undo it, Mother suddenly smiled. This was entirely unexpected since she rarely smiled even when others were smiling and, of course, the snagged hem of my coat could never have made her laugh, and there were so many different feelings contained in this smile—regret and the knowledge of the impossibility of preventing my departure, the idea of solitude and the memory of the deaths of my father and sisters, and shame before the on-coming tears, and love for me, and that whole long life which had bound Mother to me from my birth to this day—that Eka-terina Genrikhova Voronin, who was present at our parting, sud-denly covered her face with her hands and began to cry. When, finally, the door had shut behind me, the thought crossed my mind that I might never go back through that door again, and that never again would Mother cross me as she had just done, and I wanted to return home and never leave. But it was too late. The moment had already passed; I was already out on the street. walked down the street and everything that had been my life until that moment remained behind me and continued to exist without me; there was no longer any place for me here, and it was as if I had vanished.

Much later I was also to remember that it had been snowing that evening, covering the street. After two days of traveling I had come as far as Sinelnikov, where an armored train named "Smoke" was waiting to take me on as a soldier in the artillery command. It was the end of 1919; from that winter on I stopped being the gymnasium student Sosedov who was going into the seventh grade; I stopped reading books, skiing, doing gymnas-tics, going to Kislovodsk and seeing Claire; and everything that I had done up until then became for me only the vision of a mem-ory. Yet even to this new life I brought all my former habits and eccentricities; and just as at home and in school, when meaning-ful events often left me indifferent and small things which, it would seem, did not warrant much attention were particularly important to me, so too during the Civil War all the killings and injuries passed by me with hardly a trace, while several feelings and ideas, for the most part quite removed from the usual ideas one has about war, remained with me forever. My fondest mem-ory pertaining to this time was how they once sent me to an obser-vation post at the top of a tree in the middle of the woods, leaving me there alone while the armored train went several miles back to collect water. It was September, green was already turning to yellow. The enemy battery was firing on the edge of the forest where the observation post was, and the projectiles

flew across the trees with an unusual howl and a drone, something which never happens when the projectile is flying above a
field. The wind was blowing and the tops of the trees swayed
back and forth; a small squirrel with darting eyes, who was
chewing on something with those humorous, rapid jaw movements unique to rodents, suddenly noticed me, took fright, and
instantly jumped over to another tree as he straightened his fluffy
yellow tail and, for a second, remained suspended in midair.
From far off a battery was firing at the woods, and I saw only
the dull red flames of the brief flashes which came out of the
guns with each fire. The leaves rustled, somewhere down below
a grasshopper rattled, suddenly falling silent every once in a
while, as if someone were stopping his mouth with the palm of
their hand. It was so lovely and clear, and all these sounds came
to me so distinctly, and the water in the little lake which I could
see from up above flashed and rippled, that I forgot all about
having to follow the flashes and movements of the enemy cavalry, whose presence reconnaissance had communicated to us,
and that there was a Civil War going on in Russia and that I was
taking part in it.

It was during the war that I first encountered the strange
states and behavior which I would certainly never have wit-
nessed under other circumstances, and above all, I observed the
most horrible cowardice. I never felt the least bit sorry for those
who experienced this feeling, nor did I understand how a twenty-
five-year-old soldier could, during episodes of heavy shooting,
cry from fear nor how, after three six-inch missiles had fallen on
the armored train, corroding the iron walls and injuring several
people, he crawled on the floor and sobbed, crying in a piercing
voice, "Oh, my God, oh, Mama," grabbing the feet of those who
had preserved their composure. I didn't understand why this fear
suddenly communicated itself to an officer who commanded the
platform, a man usually quite courageous, who cried to the me-
chanic, "Full speed backwards!" although there was no new
danger and the projectiles of the enemy artillery were continuing
to come down around the armored train. I can not say that I
never experienced fear during times of battle; but mine was the

kind of feeling which could easily be subordinated to reason; and as there was no voluptuousness or temptation in this feeling, I didn't find it difficult to surmount. I thought that, aside from this, there was yet another reason that came into play: At this time, just as before and afterwards, I still did not possess the ability to react quickly to what was happening around me. This ability surfaced within me extraordinarily rarely, and then only when what I saw coincided with my internal state; but for the most part these were things which were to a large degree immobile and, at the same time, always distant from me; they could not excite my personal interest. Like the slow flight of a large bird, or someone's far-off whistle, or an unexpected turn of the road which opened up onto a field of reeds and a swamp, or the human eyes of a tame bear, or the cry of an unknown beast suddenly awakening me in the darkness of a dense summer night. But whenever it concerned my fate or when some danger threatened me, my peculiar form of deafness, which arose as a consequence of that same inability to respond quickly to what was happening around me, became more pronounced than ever.

It cut me off from the life of usual concerns and from the enthusiasm, characteristic of every battle condition, which breeds mental confusion. This confusion thoroughly invaded many people, cowards and brave men alike. But especially prone were simple people—peasants and rural workers; they expressed both courage and fear stronger than anyone, and went to equal degrees of despair—in some cases tranquil and in others, hysterical—as if it were one and the same feeling, only directed toward different sides. Those who were very cowardly feared death because the strength of their blind attachment to life was unusually great; those who did not fear possessed the very same awesome vital strength, since only an emotionally strong person can be courageous. But this enigmatic might clothed itself in various forms which were as unlike one another as the life of parasites and those at whose expense they feed.

And because, on the one hand, everyone who I had known and seen among my former teachers and acquaintances instilled in me throughout my life a disdain for cowardice and the duty to be courageous, and I never questioned this; and on the other hand, by virtue of the insufficient strength of my mind which could not grasp the mental state of cowards and the insufficient richness of feeling through which I might have found a similar state, I related to it with an aversion which was especially strong when the cowards were not soldiers but officers. I saw one of them who, instead of commanding the machine guns during a heavy battle, took refuge under a pile of sheepskin coats that lay inside the train; he covered his ears and did not get up until the battle had ended. Another time a second officer of the machine gun command also lay on the ground, covering his face with his palms; although it was winter and the iron floor was very cold— one's fingers nearly stuck to it—he continued to lie there for nearly two hours and didn't even catch cold, no doubt because the sheer strength of his fear had created some kind of instantaneous immunization. The third instance occurred when an enemy airplane appeared, hovering, as always, thirty miles from the edge, and began to drop bombs on the base (as the train was called where soldiers and officers coming from the front for their rotation lived—there were two shifts, one on the front lines and one at the rear; they alternated every two weeks, and in addition to these soldiers from the front there was the entire non-combat part, that is, soldiers working in the kitchen, officers holding administrative and economic posts officers' wives, clerks, intendants and about twenty women, among them laundresses, scullery maids and charwomen for the officers' wagons; these were the random women who had been picked up in various stations and who were seduced by the comforts of the base, the warm wagons, the electricity, the cleanliness, the abundant food, and the pay which they received in exchange for a few light tasks, and for that which was most needed from them, their purely female favors). Lieutenant Borschov, a sergeant-major of the armored train, looked at the sky, hastily crossed himself, gasped and crawled under the wagon on all fours, not in the least ashamed that everyone there saw him. Just then the artillerist Mikhutin, a sly muzhik and pickpocket who had never been in a battle before, leapt out of one of the wagons; he jumped down from the footboard, and without glancing to the side, ran along the field until he reached the water tower and quickly ducked inside of it. Not one of the bombs dropped on the base fell as had been anticipated; as a matter of fact, the only bomb that managed to cause any damage destroyed a part of that very water tower in which Mikhutin was hiding. As it turned out he wasn't wounded, but had been quite bruised up by the flying pieces of shattered brickwork; his fat face with its peevish, porcine expression was black and blue, his clothes were soiled with white lime, and when he returned like that everyone laughed at him. But this didn't shame him in the least since his feeling of fear was invincible. Another soldier, Tiyanov, a broad-shouldered man who could easily cross himself while holding seventy pounds of weights, was so fearful that, having come to the front for the first time and hearing the distant cannon fire, he leapt nearly eleven feet from the platform and wanted to run back to the base, but couldn't because he had dislocated his leg; he was overjoyed about this dislocated leg, since because of it they banished him to the rear of the line. One time during the shooting—he had had to go to the front nonetheless—he fell into a swoon and lay with a white face, not moving; but when I accidentally glanced at him and he had not been expecting this, I saw him quickly open his eyes and look around, then quickly close them again. But alongside such people I saw others. Colonel Pikhter, commander of the armored train "Smoke" was lying, I remember, on the roof of the platform between two rows of nuts which were used to screw different parts of the armor together. An enemy projectile slid along the iron with a scream and tore off all the fastenings formerly to the left of the colonel. He didn't even turn around, his face remained unmoved, and I didn't notice even the slightest sign of the effort he must have made to keep his composure. A senior officer of the artillery command, Lieutenant Osipov, having stepped off the platform into a field to inspect our position, landed between two chains of infantry soldiers—on one side was the chain of the Reds and on the other, the Whites. Not knowing who he was and taking him for a member of the other side, both sides began to fire on him, and from where we were you could see clouds of dust shoot up around his legs. He pressed forward nonetheless, paying no attention to the bullets; then he returned. One bullet had slightly scratched his hand. The soldier Filipenko sang quiet Ukrainian songs while a battle was going on, tried to carry on a leisurely conversation with the others, and was disappointedly surprised when, in response, he heard the reproach that he understood neither the agitation people feel nor their fear. "Weren't you afraid, Filipenko?" the commander asked him. "What's to be afraid of?" said Filipenko in surprise. "Now nighttime in a cemetery, there's something scary. But during the day nothing is frightening." But one of the bravest people I ever saw was the soldier Daniel Zhivin, whom everyone called "Danko." He was a good-natured, lean and small man, a great lover of laughter and a good comrade. He was so lacking in ambition and so able to forget himself for the sake of others that it seemed unreal. He had survived many adventures, fought in every single army that had participated in the Civil War—the Reds, the Whites, Makhno's, Hetman Skoropadsky's, Petlyura's, and even in the detachment of the Socialist-Revolutionary, Sablin, which existed for all of three days. His term on the armored train was interrupted when, along with the entire command, he was taken captive by Makhno's army, which was then at the front. The Makhnovites assigned him to a special company of infantry guarding a bridge across the Dnieper.

The bridge, one mile long, was occupied on one side by Makhno's forces and on the other by the Whites. From both ends, machine guns were firing at one another. Danko found himself at the watchpost on Makhno's side and decided to return to the armored train. He sent the relief sentry into the dugout, flung his rifle over his shoulder, and began to walk across the bridge to the other side, where the volunteers had just opened heavy fire. Nonetheless, Danko continued to move forward as though he were not moving along a narrow space pierced by ten bullets per second, but along some quiet Russian highroad leading from, say, Tula to Orel. His relief sentry, meanwhile, had grown uneasy from the sound of such unexpected fire, ran out of the dugout and, seeing Danko leaving, also opened fire on him from a second gun. Danko crossed the bridge without even being wounded. The Whites arrested him and some foolish infantry officers—two staff captains—took him for a spy and wanted to shoot him. Danko burst forth with terrible curses and exclamations invoking the Dear Lord and the apostles. This would have been no help to him, had not those standing on the platform of the armored train decided to find out what was going on. Colonel Osipov saw the ragged Danko screaming at the infantry officers and grabbed first his revolver and then his rifle. After the interception on the part of the officer from the armored train they set him free, saying never had they seen such an undisciplined officer. "You can take your discipline and . . ." cried Danko. "How is it you weren't afraid, Danko?" he was asked, after he'd been dressed and fed and was sitting by the fire in the heated goods van, smoking a cigarette made of Stambul tobacco. "Who wasn't afraid? Oh, I was afraid all right." Another time, when Danko was on his way to a reconnaissance party, he was captured again because he had gone into a village occupied by the Reds, entered a hut, started to joke with the proprietress, and asked whether there were Reds in the village—just a few moments before three Red troops had appeared unexpectedly. Danko didn't even have time to reach for his rifle. They disarmed him, locked him up in the shed, posted a guard, and sentenced Danko to death. And even then, after three days, having tracked down the base of the armored train which in the meantime had moved forty miles ahead, Danko showed up as if nothing had happened.

I was present at his conversation with the commander. "Where were you, Danko?" "I was captive." "How did you fall captive?" "The Reds arrested me." "They did nothing to you?" "No, but they wanted to shoot me." "And what did you do?" "I ran away." "How did you manage that?" "I killed the guard and ran." "And they didn't catch you?" "No," Danko said. "I ran like hell." He laughed. To me the very idea that Danko was able to kill the sentry seemed bizarre and out of keeping with his character. Evidently he had simply found it necessary; his instinct for preservation had drowned out the possibility of reflecting upon whether or not he should kill the sentry, and if Danko did not have this instinct he would have been dead a long time ago. He was, as the soldiers said of him, very young and happy-go-lucky. Once he made the entire command break out laughing when he pursued a small white piglet he had bought someplace; he ran after it for a long time, screamed at it and tried to covert he piglet with his cap; he whistled, waving his arms as he ran, and followed the animal until both he and the piglet had disappeared from sight. In the evening he returned, leading on a rope a pig which he had managed to exchange for the piglet. Everyone made fun of him and said that Danko had chased the pig for so long that it had grown up in the meantime. Danko laughed, holding his cap in his hand, his eyes cast down. He was a merry, endlessly good-natured and infinitely desperate man. "Danko, would you go to the North Pole?" I asked. "Is it interesting there?" "Very interesting. And there are lots of white bears." "Oh, no," he said, "I'm afraid of bears." "Why are you afraid of bears? They won't sentence you to death." "But they'll bite," Danko answered, and laughed. He couldn't break the habit of calling me "thou." "Danko," I explained to him, "you're a soldier just like me. Why do you call me 'thou'? Really, you know, you can speak with me as you do with Ivan." Ivan was his buddy. "I can't do that," answered Danko ashamedly. One day this same Ivan, an intelligent Ukrainian and a calm, brave soldier, asked me, "What is the Milky Way?"

"Why are you suddenly interested?"

"The soldiers asked me, 'Ivan, what in the sky is like milk?' and I said, 'the Milky Way,' only I don't know what the Milky Way is." I explained to him as best I could. The next day he came to me again.

"Tell me, please, what is the length of the circumference of a circle equal to?"

"It is determined by a special mathematical equation," I said. "I don't know if you'll understand." And I gave him the formula for the length of a circumference.

"Ah ha," he confirmed with a satisfied grin. "I tested you

on purpose, thinking you might not know. I asked the volunteer Svirsky earlier and then wrote it down and I came to test you."

He was a marvelous storyteller; I never saw anyone to compare with him among so-called intelligent people. He was quite clever and observant, and possessed the creative gift of making funny what otherwise would have not been amusing, a sense of humor without which these things always seem a bit flat. I don't remember the stories in which he displayed his astonishing imitative talents; it was precisely because they were so light and instantaneous that these stories did not leave a lasting impression; now I recalled only how he told a story with a Red general in it, when they had sent bad horses to a battery Ivan was then commanding. "I say to him," said Ivan, "'Comrade Commander, are those really chargers? The chargers are going forward and are quite astonished that they haven't keeled over yet.' And he answers, 'Thanks to the Powers that Be, not all of my commanders are as capricious as those milksops,' and I say, 'God forbid you should die, Comrade Commander, we would take you on those same horses to bury you, so don't you shake around too much.'"

I passed the time with the soldiers but around me they behaved with a certain guardedness, because I didn't understand many things which, in their opinion, were extraordinarily simple; at the same time they thought I knew things which, in turn, were inaccessible to them. I didn't know a word they used and they laughed at me because I said, "fetch water." "If you fetch water, you won't return," they remarked derisively. Nor was I able to converse with peasants; to them I seemed like some kind of Russian foreigner. Once, the commander of the platform told me I had to go into the village and buy a pig: "I should warn you," I said, "that I have never bought a pig before. Never in my life has such a case arisen; and if my purchase turns out unsuccessfully, don't say I didn't warn you." "What's this?" he answered. "Really now, you don't need Newton's binomial theory to buy a pig. No great wisdom needed here." And I set off to the village. In all the huts I stopped at, they looked at me with disbelief and a smile: "Do you have any pigs to sell?" I would ask. "What?" "Pigs." "Naw, no pigs here." I passed by forty barns and returned to the platform empty-handed. "I've come to the conclusion," I said to the officer, "that this particular variety of mammal is unknown in these parts." "And I've come to the conclusion that you simply don't know how to buy a pig," he answered. I didn't argue. Ivan, who had been present at this conversation, offered his services: "Come with me," he said to me, "and we'll buy a pig one two three." I shrugged my shoulders and went into the village a second time. At the very first hut we came to, the one where they had told me there were no pigs, Ivan bought a huge hog for half a kopek. But before doing so he chatted with the farmers about the crops, explaining that his uncle, who lives in the province of Poltava, was a close friend and neighbor of the farmer's brother-in-law; complimented them on the cleanliness of the hut—although the hut was actually rather dirty—said that there could not possibly be swine in such a farm; and asked for a drink. It ended with them feeding us to the gills, selling the hog and accompanying us to the gate. "There's your binomial," I said to the commander when I returned. And it was always the case that whenever I had to deal with peasants I never got anywhere. They did not even understand me very well, since I was unable to speak the language of simple folk, although I dearly wanted to.

On the armored train, however, there were those who had already adapted and acquired a certain polish: railway workers and telegraphists. Our soldiers were very dandified, wore "free" trousers, which was considered a free-thinking thing to do, and several of them covered their fingers with rings and signets of such gigantic proportions that no one doubted in the least that they were counterfeit. The greatest quantity of jewelry was worn by the first of the armored train scoundrels, a former butcher named Klimenko. He spent all of his free time in a state of strained attention; he kept twirling his moustache with his left hand and held his right in the air close to his eyes, the better to see the shine of his ring. His weaknesses became known after he stole money from his neighbor and got caught with it, after which the commander said to him, "Well, Klimenko, take your pick. Either stand trial and be shot like a dog, or I'll draw up the whole armored train and punch you a few times in the face in front of all of them." Klimenko fell to his knees and begged the commander to hit him in the face. Klimenko said, "in the mug." This was done the following morning and later, in the wagon, Klimenko would often recall this event and say, "I can only laugh at the stupidity of the commander." And he would actually laugh. The second scoundrel, Valentine Alexandrovich Vorobyov, was reputed to be a former officer of some small railway station. Like many elderly scoundrels, he was extraordinarily dapper. He had a fluffy beard which he carefully combed. He was very polite, sang sad Ukrainian songs in a high-pitched voice, and in spite of this, was an absolute and inveterate scoundrel. He could denounce a comrade. He could, like Klimenko, rob his own neighbor and, of course, under difficult circumstances, would betray anyone. The very same day I arrived at the armored train, he stole a box of a thousand cigarettes from me. It seemed women adored this man. He slept with all the servants and sweepers who came under his domination; once, when one of them spurned him, he wrote a denunciation in which he accused her of being a socialist; although the poor woman was illiterate, she was arrested and sent to some way station. It was winter; the woman left with her two-year-old girl in her arms. Glancing at Vorobyov, I would often wonder why women usually prefer scoundrels. Perhaps, I said to myself, it was because scoundrels are more unique than the average person; there is something in the scoundrel which is absent in others, and also because each or almost each quality carried to its extreme ceases to be seen as a normal, individual characteristic and acquires the magnetic strength of an exception; and so, despite the fact that my former life had ended, I still had not altogether departed from it; I retained several school habits. I was still a schoolboy and my thoughts would acquire a special bent in advance, condemning to barrenness and disparity those original thoughts which, however, served only as a pretense for my fantasy's return to its favorite places. Women loved hangmen: The historical crimes which took place hundreds of years ago had, to this day, not lost their thrilling appeal for these women. And why nor assume that

Vorobyov was a miniature of grandiose crimes? But this was absurd and did not come to anything. Vorobyov occupied himself with stealing sugar and manufactured goods from neighboring trains, and one night, tinkering with the engine, he managed to drive a new second-class yellow wagon away from the train belonging to the commander of the front, General Tryasunov. But in the evening, lying on his bunk bed with a face pale from drunkenness and hazy, sorrowful eyes, he still complained that the will of fate had forced him to take part in the Civil War.

"My God," he would say, nearly in rears, "what a situation. People shot, hanged, killed, tortured. Why on earth am I here? Whom did I wrong? What is it all for? Dear God, I wish I were home. I have a wife. My small children ask, 'Where is Papa?' And papa sits here beneath the gallows. What shall I say to the children?" he cried. "Where is my justification? There's one consolation: We're going to Alexandrovsk. I'll go to my wife and surprise her at night. I'll say, 'Are you tired of waiting for me, dear? Well, here I am.'"

And Alexandrovich Vorobyov actually did go to his wife, and returned appeased. But when we had gone forty versts and were staying in a small station for a few days, he complained once again, "My God, what a situation. People shot, hanged, for what?" he cried once more. "The children will ask, 'Where were you, Papa?' What shall I tell them?" He was silent, sighed, and then said pensively, "I've got it. Let's go to Melitopol, I'll go see my wife. I'll be home again. 'What,' I'll say, 'tired of waiting for me, dear? Well here I am.'"

"But is your wife already in Melitopol?" I asked. He looked at me with unseeing, drunken eyes which expressed tender emotion and gratitude.

"Yes, dear friend, in Melitopol."

But once we had left Melitopol, he would continue to dream about how he would return to his wife, now as far as Dzhankoi.

"Brother, you've quite a treasure for a wife," the others said to him mockingly. "Not a wife, but an omnipresent Virgin Mary. How is it possible that she's in Alexandrovsk and Melitopol and in Dzhankoi, and everywhere there are children and apartments?

You've got a nice little arrangement there." And then Vorobyov gave an explanation which evidently seemed entirely adequate to him, although it surprised everyone else.

"Children," he said, "well, you know, I'm a railway man."

"Well, so what does that mean?"

"Fools," said Vorobyov in amazement. "Apparently, you don't know the fate of a railway worker. There's a wife in every city, my dears, in every city."

The third scoundrel was Paramonov, a student who, not long before my arrival, was slightly wounded in the leg. He never actually caused anyone any harm, but every day, two hours before the doctors' rounds, he would rub butter in his wound to prevent it from healing; he was therefore thought to be wounded an endlessly long time and did not go to the front. Everyone saw and knew what he'd done, but treated him with silent contempt and disgust, and no one could get up the nerve to tell him that he shouldn't do that. He was always alone and everyone avoided speaking to him; usually he sat in his corner and, looking around furtively, ate lard and bread. He was very gluttonous. He lived like a solitary animal whose presence, though unpleasant, is tolerated. He was silent and hostile to everyone, and when passersby would cross his bunk he would follow them with a suspicious and evil look. A while later he was ordered somewhere else. I remembered Paramonov several years later when I was already out of the country: I saw a dying eagle owl bound tight to a tree with a twisted rope; as soon as he heard the steps, the owl straightened himself, his feathers puffed up, he waved his wings slowly and clacked his beak; his blind, malicious yellow eyes looked straight ahead. On the train there were liars, swindlers—there was even one evangelist who came from who knows where, installed himself in our wagon and lived without a care in the world, preaching nonresistance to evil. "I have never come near your rifle and shall never touch it," he said. "It is a sin." "And if you're attacked?" "I will repel them with words." But one time, when he had taken a mess-tin of borscht and another filled with kasha for dinner and it was slyly snatched from him, he flew into a rage, grabbed—by a strange coincidence—the very rifle which he had sworn never to touch, and would have caused quite a tragedy had he not been disarmed.

But the most surprising man I came across in the war was the soldier Kopchik, distinguishable externally by his invincible laziness. He couldn't bear the least bit of work and did everything with great pains and sighs, although he was perfectly healthy and strong. Because of his incessant evasion of duties the soldiers were not overly fond of him, since they had to take up much of the slack. He always lived as if in hiding, filled with the fear that they would force him to load flour into the wagons, carry water, or peel potatoes. He sometimes walked past the base, and as soon as he did, his unshaven chin and tearful eyes, and his whole figure in its frayed and dirty service jacket and equally worn-out trousers would disappear; even the bloodhounds couldn't find him. He tried not to go to the front for the same reason he was hiding in the base: One had to work there, too. But if you were in the rear, there was the chance of evading it, something which became impossible on the platform or in battle. The sloth of this soldier was immeasurably stronger than his fear of death, because he didn't fully understand the sense of danger; work, on the other hand, (as he understand perfectly well) kept him from the two things he loved more than anything on earth—idleness and day-dreaming. I could not imagine a situation in which Kopchik would suddenly show even a part of his huge energy, which he spent in thinking up ways to shun work and in lengthy reposes beneath the wagons, where he would lie in hot summer weather. I didn't know if Kopchik was able to perform even a paltry task, one that would somehow indicate that he thought about why he was living and the reasons for the long reflections which usually filled up his idleness. And then once, on the platform, during a heavy battle, while Kopchik was taking the projectiles from their beds and handing them with terror in his eyes to the gunlayer—every projectile was accompanied by a plaintive sigh and after the fifth he said, "My back is hurting. These projectiles are really heavy"—just then enemy grenades tore over our cannon. The gunlayer, wounded in the abdomen, fell to the ground and the cannon stopped firing. In the instantly ensuing confusion no one knew what to do, and only Kopchik, who saw that he would no longer have to work, sighed with relief, slapped his hand on the still burning-hot cannon and, startled, went up to the wounded man practically leaping up and down. Blood was flowing onto the ground. The final panic of death was on the wounded man's face. "You won't die," Kopchik said to him amidst general silence. From far off, at equal intervals, came the sound of four cannon shots. "Look how healthy you are," he calmly continued. "Your blood is very red—a sick man's blood is blue." "My heart won't take it," said the gunlayer. "Your heart?" repeated Kopchik. "That's not true, your heart is strong. If it were weak, then of course it wouldn't endure. Now I'll tell you about a weak heart. Once when I was going to bathe my horse I saw a water sprite not far off, looking very sad." The gunlayer looked at Kopchik with an effort. "'Well,' I thought, 'I'll give it a scare.' And I did. I cried, 'What are you doing here, wattles?' And he died of fright, because he had a weak heart. But you've got a very strong heart." But before we had reached the base the gunlayer died; and when, three days later I was walking along and spotted Kopchik's tangled hair beneath the wagon, I felt strange and troubled in my soul, and I quickly moved away from him; there was something inhuman and evil about this soldier, something I would not have wanted to know. But my attention was soon distracted by a quarrel the chief cook at an officers' meeting—located in a special Pullman wagon—was having with the armored train's shoeshiner, a beautiful fifteen-year-old boy named Vasily who, being the lover of a certain no-longer-young and lame woman, had cheated on her either with a laundress or with a scullery maid; the whole time she scolded him with uncensored words, and three soldiers who were standing not far off were laughing heartily. Romances took up much of the officers', as well as many of the enterprising soldiers' time; the maids quickly understood their own worth and put on airs. One of them, a strong woman from Yaroslav named Katyusha, didn't want to know anyone, and did not yield to persuasion until she had been paid first: The resident teller of drawing-room jokes, Lieutenant Dirgach, complained about her to everyone:

"No, my dear Sir Lieutenant," said Katyushka proudly, "I'm not sleeping with anyone now for free. Give me the ring from your finger and I'll sleep with you." Dirgach wavered for a long time. "You don't understand," he said, "This ring was a sacred gift from my fiancée." But love, as he put it, won out, and Lieutenant Dirgach doesn't have a ring any more, unless he has bought another one. But the most inaccessible woman on the armored train was a nurse, a haughty woman who acted with great disdain towards the soldiers and only rarely condescended to have scornful conversations with them. I remembered how, one evening, I was lying in my bunk as she was dressing Paramonov's wounds, having brought him into my sleeping compartment earlier because I had a brighter electric lamp; she raised her head and saw my face. "What a young one," she said. "What province are you from?" "Petersburg, sister." "Petersburg? How did you manage to get to the south?" "I just came." "What did you do before that? Were you a peddlar?" "No, sister. I studied." "In a parish school?" "No, sister, not in a school." "Well, then, where?" "In a gymnasium," I said and, unable to contain myself, burst out laughing. She blushed. "What grade were you in?" "The seventh, respected sister." Later she avoided me, and looked at me only from afar.

Just as, in order to remember clearly and distinctly my life in the military school and the incomparable, stony sorrow with which I left that tall building, I had only to imagine the taste of the meatballs, the meat sauce and macaroni—so could I, as soon as I smelled burnt coal, immediately picture the beginning of my service on the armored train, the winter of 1919, snow-covered Sinelnikov, the bodies of the Makhnovites hanging from the telegraph poles, their frozen bodies swinging in the winter wind and striking the wood of the poles with a blunt, light sound, the blackening hamlets behind the station, the whistle of the engines sounding like distress signals, and the white summit of the rails, incomprehensible in their motionlessness. It seemed to me that they were rushing ahead quivering at the joints, as if mutely

speaking of a distant voyage through the snow and the black settlements of Russia, through winter and war, to unusual countries
reminiscent of huge aquariums filled with water, which one
could breathe like air, and music which shook the green surface;
beneath the surface stirred the long stems of plants, and behind
the glass unreal animals floated by on the leaves of waterlilies—
I could not picture them but I could not stop feeling their existence each time I looked at the rails and the sleeper car
half-covered with snow, like the planks of an endlessly long fence
turned upside down. And there is still one more thing which I
owe to staying on the armored train: the feeling of perpetual departure. The base went from one place to another; those objects
which constantly and unmovingly surrounded me—my books,
suits, a few engravings, the electric lamp above my head—would
suddenly begin to move and at this moment I would understand
the idea of movement, and the ruling nature of this idea, more
clearly than I ever had before. I could want or not want to leave;
but already the lamp would have begun to shake, the books
would leap up and down on the shelf, the carbine that was hung
up would scurry along the wooden wall, and beyond the wall
the snow-covered earth was spinning and the light from the base
window quickly ran across the field which rose up, then fell,
leaving behind it a long, right-angled streak of space, a road
from these countries into other ones.

As it left the station the train quickened its pace, and
through the window the withered legs hanging in white under-
pants, which the wind blew like the sails of a ship caught in a
storm, flew by. Those most complex interlacings of the many
reasons which forced me, during the winter of that year, to find
myself on the armored train going south at night—reasons which
have already ceased to exist since no one's memory could pre-
serve them—have vanished long ago; but this voyage still con-
tinues within me and most likely until the day I die I will, from
time to time, feel myself lying on the upper bunk of my compartment and see, through the lit windows as I traversed both
space and time, the quick flash of the hanged men carried beneath white sails into non-being; once again the snow will begin

to spin and that shadow of a vanished train flying through the long years of my life will start to slip, bobbing up and down. And perhaps the reason I always briefly regretted leaving people and countries, perhaps this feeling of only very fleeting regret was evanescent precisely because nothing that I saw and loved—soldiers, officers, women, snow and war—will ever leave me, not until the time has come for my last deathly voyage, the slow fall into the black abyss, a million times more protracted than my earthly existence, so long that while I am falling I will have time to forget about everything that I have seen and remembered and felt and loved; and when I have forgotten everything that I have loved, then I will die.

And the last companion to be forgotten will be Arkady Savin. He was a unique fellow who resembled people alive in my imagination, and a wonderful twentieth-century force transformed him into a conquistador, a romantic and a bard, as though having plucked his broad-shouldered shadow from the gloomy expanses of the Middle Ages. He served with us and went to the front just as we did, but everything he did was exceptional and unusual. In a battle with Makhno's infantry, when only two men out of fourteen were left on the platform of the armored train—the rest had been killed or wounded—Arkady, who had a disfiguring contusion of the jaw, stepped onto the dead body of another man, whose head had been blown off and whose headless body still twitched, his already inhuman, separate fingers still clawing the ground. And Arkady, soiling his service jacket in the human brains, took up the cannon alone and fired for a long time at the Makhnovites, who were clambering onto the embankment. His bravery was not the usual bravery: All of Arkady's deeds were characterized by accuracy, unreal speed, and confidence. And it appeared that his own awareness of his immeasurable superiority over others never left him. His movements during times of danger were quick, like the movements of a Japanese juggler or acrobat. Overall there was something Asiatic about Arkady, a part of that mysterious spiritual might which people of the yellow race possess and which is inscrutable to white people. At the same time, Arkady was heavy and big. The officers could not forgive him for those disdainful grins which he offered in response to their lame orders during battle. When the armored train went to the front and the platform, weighing several tons, rolled irrepressibly along the rails, quivering and rumbling, the figure of Arkady standing in front and looking ahead of him, although there was nothing unexpected or unusual about this pose, looked to me like a gloomy statue on a vehicle of war. This is how he appeared to me at the front. In the rear he became different.

He loved to dress well, drank a lot, would always go to the city or the settlements around the base, and at night we would be awakened by the distant peals of his resonant baritone. He always sang when he was returning. He generally sang very well; he really knew what music was. With a pale face and head leaning on his chest, he would sit for long moments in the compartment without moving, and then suddenly a deep, chesty sound would fill the train: after a moment I would lose sight of the walls of the wagons with the rifles hanging along them, the books and lamp, and my friends, as if none of this had ever existed and everything I had known up until then had been a horrible mistake, and there would be nothing on earth besides this voice and Arkady's white face and laughing eyes, even though he always sang sad, wistful songs. And at the same moment I would think that there were no bad sorrowful songs and that if some had bad words, then it was because I didn't know how to understand them, because, listening to a naive song, I could not wholeheartedly give myself over to it and forget those aesthetic habits which my upbringing had created in me, not having taught me the precious art of self oblivion. More often than anything else Arkady sang a romance whose verse form might, at another time, have called forth only a smile from me; but had I been able to notice the insufficiencies of this form during Arkady's singing, I would have become a thousand times more unhappy than I already was. I never heard this romance from anyone again:

I am lonely and time flees so quickly.
The days, the weeks, the years rush by,
But happiness only comes to me in dreams
I never see it in real life.

Now soon, very soon in the sea of life
My canoe will disappear.
Listen to the last reproach,
And you will understand how lonely I am.
Listen to the last reproach,
And you will understand how lonely I am. . .

Soldiers, officers and the armored train's women would gather beneath the window of the wagon. In the summer he would sing in the evening, and his voice was lost in the far-off and burning silence of the dark air. Arkady sang this song even on the days when the small lakes of Sivasha had already turned blue and we were on our last digression. We had left Tavrya; standing at the window, Arkady kept singing about the canoe and the train hummed, its iron wheels gnashed and vanished in clouds of prickly dust; and the plump domes of a church would disappear and then pop up again before us.

Arkady often had dreams; shortly before this retreat, a mermaid came to him in a dream. She was laughing and she beat her tail as she swam up to him, pressing her cold body against him, her scales glittering blindingly. I remembered Arkady's dream when, late one night in Sevastopol, I saw a motorboat on the ocean waves of the Black Sea that was quickly moving towards a huge English cruiser standing on the roadstead. The boat raised behind itself a glittering crest of water, and it suddenly seemed to me that I could hear barely audible laughter reaching me through this water, and an unbearable shine appeared through the dark blue.

For a whole year the armored train went along the rails of Tavra and the Crimea, like a wild animal, a beast surrounded by a circle of hunters. It changed directions, went forward, then returned, then went to the left, only to rush back again after a while. To the south, the sea unfolded before us. In the north, armed Russia stood barring the road, and all around us in the windows revolved fields which were green in summer, white in winter, and always deserted and hostile. The armored train went everywhere, and in the summer it arrived in Sevastopol. There were white lime roads passing above the sea and clay mountains towered along the shore; small pochards flew and then fell headlong into the water. On forgotten piers stood rusty battleships; near their sides, which sunk down low into the water, seahorses leapt, black crabs moved sideways along the bottom, glassy fish swam past as if blind; and in the black hollow of the underwater ground lazy gobies stood, immobile. It was very hot and quiet, and it seemed to me that in this sunny quiet, above the blue sea, some transparent deity was expiring in the bright air.

Life at this time felt as if it were being lived in three different countries: the country of summer, quiet and the lime heat of Sevastopol; the country of winter, with its snow and storms; and the country of our nighttime history, night alarms and battles and whistles in the dark and cold. It was different in each of these countries, and with each country we came to we brought the others with us. On cold nights, standing on the iron floor of the armored train, I would see before my eyes the sea and the lime; in Sevastopol the sunshine reflecting off an unseen wall would suddenly transport me to the north. But it was especially the country of night which was unlike anything I had known in my life up until then. I remembered how at night the mournful, drawn-out whine of bullets would slowly pass above our heads. And all of this involuntary awakening of the air, this uneasy and unsure movement of sounds in the air, was made especially strange by the fact that, while the bullet flew very quickly, its sound slid melancholically and unhurriedly. Occasionally one could hear the quick sound of an alarm coming from the village; red clouds that, until then, had been invisible in the darkness would be lit up by the flames of the fire, and people would run out of their houses with the kind of trepidation sailors must feel when they run out onto the deck of a ship which has sprung a leak in the open sea, far from shore. At the time I often thought about ships, as if I were rushing to live out the life which had been destined for me later on, when we would rock up and down on a steamboat in the Black Sea half-way between Russia and the Bosphorus.

There was a good deal of unreality in the contrived union of the diverse people who fired the cannons and machine guns: They moved along the ground of southern Russia, rode on horseback, whizzed along in trains, perished, crushed under the wheels of retreating artillery, died and stirred, dying and vainly attempting to fill the huge space of sea, air and snow with a meaning which was not God's but somehow their own. And the simplest soldiers who remained in this situation—the same Ivanovs and Sidorovs who were dreamers and idlers—these people suffered from the untruth and unnaturalness of what was happening more than the rest, and perished sooner than the others.

So, for example, perished the armored train barber Kostyuchenko, a young soldier, drunkard and dreamer. He cried at night, always dreaming of fires and horses and engines on cog-wheels. All day long, from morning to night, he sharpened his razor, uttering cries and laughing to himself. People began to avoid him. Then one fine day, as he was shaving a commander of the armored train, in whose presence a soldier was not sup-posed to talk, he suddenly began to sing a tongue-twisting, danc-ing motif with unexpectedly abrupt sounds characteristic of several soldiers' songs:

> Oy, Oy!
> I go to the tavern,
> An old woman lies on her side,
> Asleep.

He wailed on without cease, and with habitual mechanical movements he shaved the instantly reddening cheeks of the com-mander. Then he lay the razor to the side, shoved two fingers into his mouth and began to whistle piercingly. He grabbed the razor again and cut the curtains on the window to shreds. They took him out of the commander's compartment and for a long time didn't know what to do with him. Finally they decided, and shoved him into an empty goods wagon from one of those innumerable trains which brought, Lord knows why or where, the corpses of soldiers who had died from typhus and the leaping bodies of the sick who had not yet managed to die. The sick lay on straw, and the wooden floor with its numerous cracks trembled along with them—no matter where the train went, they died anyway. And after days of traveling, the bodies of the sick made only those dead movements which came from the jolts of the train, as happened with the carcasses of horses which had been killed, or with animals. They carried Kostyuchenko off in this empty wagon; no one found out what happened to him after that. I imagined his shining eyes in the darkness of the tightly-locked goods wagon, and the inscrutable state of his dim mind in which, somewhere, there still flickered the distant consciousness which the mad retain. But the case of Kostyuchenko was the last one pertaining to the time we were in the pre-frontal region, because after a long winter in the blue-ice mirrors of Sivasha and that continuous view of the sandy dike with its black sleeper cars, the red lights of Semaphore, the pot-bellied water towers filled with frozen water which we saw as we spent days and weeks "approaching the Crimea," and after Dzhankoi, where our base stayed for a long time, we left and went deep into the country. We remained for a long while in Dzhankoi, with its dark houses where officers wives, like so many Messalinas, took shelter. They had been without husbands for a long time and would come into our cars to drink vodka, eat steak, and take food from the station buffet; and, when sated, they would endlessly fidget by the seats of the compartment with hiccups of wearied greed. With quick, unnoticed movements they unfastened their threadbare dresses and would later cry and scream in passion and after two minutes would cry once more, but this time with more touching and transparent tears, and bemoan, as they said, the past. Their regret suddenly painted in fantastic, festive colors their obscure life in the provinces, married to a lieutenant captain, a drunkard and gambler; it seemed to them that they hadn't understood their meagre happiness and that their life had been good and pleasant; however, they did not possess the art of remembering, and all of them always told, in more or less the same words, how on Easter night they would walk with lit candles and how the bells rang out. I never saw such women before the war or the armored train. They spoke in war-time words and expressions, carried themselves loosely, especially after they had satisfied their hunger, slapped men on the hands and winked at them. Their knowledge was amazingly sparse; their awful spiritual poverty and the vague idea that their lives could be different made them unbalanced; as a type they most of all resembled prostitutes, but prostitutes with recollections. Only one of these women, now inseparable from my memory of the sofas dirty velvet, the Dzhankoi kerosene lamps and the even slices of marinated herring we ate with wine and vodka, Eliza veta Mikhailovna, was different from her girlfriends. Somehow it always happened that she would visit us while I was asleep—either around nine in the morning or two at night. They would wake me up and say, "Wake up, you're in the way, Eliza veta Mikhailovna has come," and this name woke me in an instant; after some time had gone by, Eliza veta Mikhailovna became an involuntary companion in my dreams. "Elizaveta Mikhailovna," I heard, and fell back asleep, and then once more, "Eliza veta Mikhailovna." Opening my eyes I would see a not overly tall, thin woman with a big, red mouth and laughing eyes; it looked as if blue sparks were dancing on the yellow skin of her face. She looked like a foreigner. I would never have known anything about her had I not, waking up one time, overheard her conversation with one of my colleagues, the philologist Lavinov. They spoke about literature, and in a singsong voice she read poetry, and by the sound of her voice it was evident that she was sitting and rocking slightly back and forth. Lavinov was the most educated person among us; he loved Latin and often read me Caesar's Commentaries, which I listened to out of politeness, since I had studied them in school not long before; as with everything I was forced to learn, it had become dull and uninteresting; but to Lavinov's love for the laconic and Caesar's precise language was added a predilection for the melancholy lyrics of Korolenko, and even several stories by Kuprin. More than anything, however, he loved Garshin. But in spite of such strange taste he always completely understood everything he read, and his understanding exceeded his own emotional capacities; this gave his conversations a particular sense of uncertainty. His knowledge, however, was rather extensive. He would say in his deep voice, "Yes, Elizaveta Mikhailovna, that's how it is. Bad."

"Yes, bad."

Thus the conversation would continue for a rather long time—all about what was good or not good, and it seemed that they knew no other words. But Elizaveta Mikhailovna did not leave; one could hear in her tone that, in answer to every "good" or "bad" uttered by Lavinov, something important and having nothing to do with this conversation was going on inside her, something singularly meaningful for both her and for Lavinov. It is the same when someone is drowning and above him bubbles appear on the surface of the water; the person who didn't see the drowning man go under notices only the bubbles and gives them no meaning; and all the while under the water a man is choking and dying, and it is through these bubbles that his whole, long life, with all its many feelings, impressions, pity and love, departs. The same happened with Elizaveta Mikhailovna: "Good" or "bad"—these were only bubbles on the surface of the conversation. Then I heard her start to cry, and Lavinov speaking to her in a quivering voice; then they both left. She didn't visit us any more, and it was only just before our departure that I saw her with Lavinov at the station; I was sitting at a table opposite them and, after I had eaten my fourth meat pie, Eliza veta Mikhailovna began to laugh and said, turning to Lavinov, "Don't you find that your sleeping bunkmate, when he's awake, has a wonderful appetite?" Lavinov glanced at her with eyes glassy from happiness, and answered affirmatively to all her questions. Elizaveta Mikhailovna was dressed neatly: She had an air of confidence and contentment and now, when she was apparently happy, I suddenly felt regret, as if it would have been better for her to have remained just as she was before, when I would see her in a dream as I woke up and fell back asleep again, hearing this grouping of names: "Elizaveta Mikhailovna, Eliza-veta Mikhailovna!" It did not cease being a woman's name but became for me one of my own states, lodged between the dark spaces of a dream and the red velvet of the divans which appeared in front of me just as I opened my eyes.

After Dzhankoi and winter, Sevastopol rose up in my memory, covered with white stony dust, the immobile green of Primorsky Boulevard and the bright sand of its alleys. The waves beat against the slab of the piers and, as they roll out, uncover the green stones where moss and seaweed grow; the seaweed paddles helplessly in the water, and its dripping stalks are like the branches of a willow; battleships stand on the road, and the eternal landscape of the sea, the mast and the white seagulls live and flutter as they do everywhere there is a sea, jetties and ships, and where now rise the stone lines of houses built on the yellow sandy expanse, from which the ocean retreats. It was more keenly felt in Sevastopol than anywhere else that we were living out the last days of our stay in Russia. Boars sailed in and out. English and French soldiers left the shore, and their ships passed out of sight into the sea. And it seemed that it would have been impossible to return from out there back to Russia; it seemed the sea was always the entrance to our native land, which was far from these places, on the maps of tropical countries with their straight trees and even, square patches of green land; and what was normally thought to be native—the dry heat of southern Russia, the arid fields and salty, Asiatic lakes was only a delusion. Once I killed a pochard with my rifle; it hovered on the waves for a long time and each moment, it seemed, was just about to float to shore when the coastal tide would draw it out again. I left only when it had grown dark and I could no longer see the pochard. With such helplessness did we, too, waver on the surface of events; it drew us farther and farther away until, having had to leave the zone of Russian gravity, we found ourselves in the region of other, more eternal influences and floated without romance or sails on a black-coal steamboat away from the Crimea, from all the vanquished soldiers who had turned into ragged and hungry people. But this happened somewhat later; in the spring and summer of 1920, I wandered about Sevastopol, going into cafés and theaters and amazing "Eastern cellars," where *chebureks* and yoghurt were eaten, where swarthy Armenians gazed with Olympic tranquility at the drunken tears of the officers as they swallowed down horrendous alcoholic concoctions and sang "God save the Tsar" in unsteady voices. The song sounded both indecent and sad, as it had long since lost its meaning and died away in the Eastern cellar where, from the Petersburg barracks, the musical grandeur of the ruined empire had come; it slid along the sooty walls and got stuck between the Georgian breasts of naked beauties, drawn with broad flanks, equine eyes and the unusually even, wooden drifts of tobacco smoke coming out of hookahs. All the sorrow of provincial Russia, all her eternal melancholy, pervaded Sevastopol. In the theaters, Odessan artists with aristocratic pseudonymns sang romances in bellowing voices which, completely independent of their contents, sounded extraordinarily wistful; they met with great success. I saw tears in the eyes of usually unsentimental people. Having deprived them of their homes, families and dinner parties, the Revolution had suddenly given them the ability to feel deep regret, and for an instant liberated from their coarse, warlike casing their long-forgotten, long-lost emotional sensitivity. It was as if these people were taking part in a minor-keyed symphony of the theater hall; they saw for the first time that there was a biography and a history to their lives, and a lost happiness which they had only read about in books. And the Black Sea seemed to me like a huge basin of Babylonian rivers, and the clay hills of Sevastopol—the ancient wailing wall. Hot, airy waves rolled across the small town and suddenly the wind began to blow, lifting a ripple on the water and once again reminding me of my inevitable departure. People were already talking of exit passports and beginning to pack their things; but not long after this, the armored train was sent to the front again, and we left, glancing back at the sea, plunging into dark tunnels and once again returning to those hostile Russian expanses which we had managed to get out of with such difficulty just the winter before. This was the last attack of the White army: It didn't last long, and soon the troops were running along the frozen war roads to the south once more. During those months the fate of the army interested me even less than it had before. I didn't think about it; I traveled on the platform of the armored train past burnt-out fields and yellowed trees, past groves which grew along the rails; and in the fall they sent me to a command post in Sevastopol, now slightly changed, since it was already the beginning of October. There I nearly drowned, sailing in a rotten motor boat from the northern to the southern side of the bay during a storm. After staying in Sevastopol for several days, I returned to the armored train which, in my imagination, was just as I had left it, though it had long ago been siezed by the Red Army's detachment. The base had also fallen into their hands and its command had scattered, and only three dozen soldiers and officers had somehow managed to retreat along with the remaining troops. They stayed together in one heated goods wagon and were being jolted up and down, looking dully at the red walls and not yet fully understanding that there was no longer any armored train nor any army, that Chub, our best gunlayer, had been killed, that Filipenko, whose leg had been cut off, had died, that Vanya the sailor, who knew how to curse in the most intricate fashion, was now in captivity, and that the entire supply section of the train—the section led by the artillery man Mikhutin, one turkey, one live pig, calves and horses, all in that wonderful zoological state to which they had grown accustomed—also no longer existed. One of my comrades, Lapchin, who had not left and was playing the "Funeral March" and then "The Apple" in the heated goods wagon, was saying lightheartedly, "If the turkeys and swine died without having endured this turning point in history, then we must have perished a long time ago . . . We can only keep on going."

Many stayed on, not wanting to retreat. Some went back north to the Red Army, and in one of the meeting cars they caught sight of Vorobyov in his railroad cap with its red top. He was slowly leaving, threatening with his fist, and in a long, drawn-out voice he cried, "Swine! Swine!" as if he were on a raft, rowing along a river bank, and he was straining his voice the way one has to strain to be heard on a river or lake.

The train I took to meet up with the departing troops stopped in a small station and went no further. No one knew why the train had stopped. Then I heard the conversation of some officer or other with the trainmaster. The officer was saying rapidly, "No, you tell me why we're standing here. No, I ask you, what the devil are we stuck here for? No, I won't stand for this, you know. No, you answer me." "We can't go further. There are Reds to the rear of us," answered a second voice. "In the rear? That's not ahead. If it were ahead then certainly we couldn't go. You know, we're not moving backwards, to the rear, get it? The devil take it!" "I'm not starting this train." "Why not?" "The Reds are behind us." After that, vicious cursing could be heard, and then the trainmaster said in a whining voice, "I can't go, there are Reds behind us." He repeated this phrase because he was seized by a deathly fear, and it seemed to him that no matter where he went, everywhere one and the same fate awaited him: He had ceased understanding, and was simply babbling unconsciously like an animal that is being pulled along on a string. So the train never went anywhere. I passed over to one of the wagons from the base of a light armored train called "The Wise Yaroslav," which was also standing there. And as I hadn't slept for two nights, the moment I lay down on a cot I immediately fell asleep. In a dream I saw Elizaveta Mikhailovna, who had changed into a Spanish woman with crackling castanets. She was dancing, completely naked, to the music of an unusually noisy orchestra; within the noise, the loudest of all was the deep boom of the contrabass and the sharp, high sound of a French horn. The noise became intolerable, and when I opened my eyes I heard the roar of a miniature bear who, dragging its long chain along the ground, was tossing back and forth along the wagon. Occasionally it would stop and begin to rock from side to side. There was no one in the wagon besides myself, the bear and some peasant woman in a shawl; God knows how or why she got there—and she was very frightened. She screamed loudly and cried. It was just beginning to grow light outside. The windows jingled and fell out. The wind blew: The base of the armored train was being heavily machine-gunned.

"Budyonny!" cried the peasant woman. "Budyonny!"

Not far from us the six-pound guns of a naval battery thundered heavily, answering the fire of the Red artillery. I came out onto the wagon platform and saw a grey mass of Budyonny cavalry a quarter of a mile from the base. There were groans and the roar of cannons in the air. Nearby, we could hear a flying middle-range missile, and by the sound it made it was easy to predict that the missile would drop on our or a neighboring wagon; and that's why the old woman fell silent, unconsciously submitting to the feeling of emotional and physical silence which precedes the moment of a horrible event, and I understood that she, knowing nothing about those differing tones of whizzing grenades by which an artillerist can hear where, approximately, the explosion will go off, felt a horrible danger threatening her. But the missile dropped on the neighboring wagon which was packed with wounded officers; at once there came an entire wave of cries, as in a concert when the conductor, with a quick gesture, suddenly thrusts his wand into the right or left wing of the orchestra, and from there an entire fountain of sound instantly rises, along with the wavering of strings. The six-inch weapons kept sending missile after missile directly into the black mass of people and horses, and pieces of black debris floated visibly in the pillars of smoke raised by the explosions. I stood on the platform of the wagon and gazed in front of me, freezing in the sixteen degree cold, and I dreamed about the warm bunk back at the base of my armored train, the electric lamp, the books, the hot shower, and the warm bed. I knew that the part of the train where I found myself was surrounded by Budyonny's cavalry, that it was "cut off," that there were enough missiles for another couple of hours, and that sooner or later, but not later than that evening, we would be killed or taken prisoner. I knew this perfectly well, but the dream about the warmth and the white sheets so preoccupied me that I had no time to think about anything else; or rather, this dream was more pleasant and delightful than any other possible thoughts, and I could not part with it. The black rain from the explosions and the different sounds—from the dry scratch of a bullet against stone and the resilient sound of rails and wagon wheels, to the thin peal of the cannon fire and human cries—all of this merged into one noise but did not blend, and each series of sounds retained its own existence. All this continued from early in the morning until three or four in the afternoon. I returned to the wagon, left it once again, unable either to get warm or to fall asleep, and finally I saw black spots on the horizon which were approaching the battlefield. "The Red Cavalry!" someone shouted. "It's the end!" But the cannons and machine guns kept on firing without stop, once in a while subsiding like a strong downpour which would renew itself after the first gust of wind. An old officer, an intendant colonel with a tearful face, walked passed me several rimes, apparently nor knowing where he was going or why. Some soldier got under the wagon and rolled a cigarette with fingers blue from cold, immediately exuding a whole cloud of burning Makhorka smoke. "The bullets won't reach here, brother," he said to me with a smile when I had bent down to look at him. But suddenly the battle slackened. The shooting grew sparser. The cavalry was approaching from the north. Having climbed onto the roof of the train, I could clearly make out the horses and horsemen, a thick charge of which was coming towards us in a trot. Hiding between two buffers, the old colonel was crying; next to him, clutching the end of his yellow hood, stood an eight-year-old girl all bundled up; the smoke from the cigarette of the smoking soldier, which seemed to be coming out of the ground, was quickly carried off by the wind. Soon the clip-clop of the horses' hooves could be heard and, after a few minutes of agonizing waiting, as in the theater, hundreds of riders came quite near to us. The mass of Budyonny's cavalry began to stir. The sound of cries reached us, and after a short time everything began to move; Budyonny's army started to retreat. The cavalry which had come from the north followed after them. Not far from me an officer in a Circassian coat galloped by, turning around and yelling something. And I saw that not only did the soldiers following him understand nothing, but he himself did not know why he was yelling or what it was he wanted to say. Right after this I saw the old colonel who had just been crying. Now he went to his van with an important and business-like expression on his face; the smoke beneath the wagon had ceased. The soldier emerged, cried to me, "Well, thank the Lord," and ran off somewhere to the side.

After a whole day of roaming among the endless wagons, goods vans and a string of carts, I found those forty people who continued to call themselves the armored train "Smoke," even though the armored train no longer existed. The army dwindled with each hour: Its carts rattled along the icy road, the army was vanishing into the horizon, and its noise and movements were carried off by the strong wind. This took place on the 16th and 17th of October; on the 20th of the same month, when I was sitting in a village hut not far from Feodosiya and eating bread with jam, washing it down with hot milk in a room filled with excited and smiling faces, in walked my colleague Mitya Marquis. He was called this because once, when he was asked what book out of all those he had read he liked the best, he named a novel by an unknown but undoubtedly good French writer, and the novel was entitled *The Destitute Countess*. I read this novel because Mitya had brought it with him. Its main characters were people of title; Mitya could not read such books without emotion, although he himself was a native of the Yekaterinoslav province and had never seen a big city, nor had the slightest idea what France was like, but such words as "marquis," "countess," and especially "baron" were filled with deep meaning for him and so he was called Marquis. "They've taken Dzhankoi," said Mitya-Marquis, with the delight he always felt even in those circumstances when he communicated the most horrible news. Every event aroused in him the happy feeling that he, Mitya-Marquis, had been left unharmed once more; once such important things began to happen, then something even more interesting would follow. I remembered that in the most difficult circumstances, even if someone had been killed or fatally wounded, Mitya-Marquis would say with excitement, panting in order to hide his laughter: "Filipenko's leg was torn off and Chernusov was wounded in the abdomen, and the gunlayer

Sanin was wounded in the left arm: Onward, Fate!" "They've taken Dzhankoi, that spells bad news," said Mitya. Actually Dzhankoi was on this side of those fortifications which had already reached the Crimea. Dzhankoi: The kerosene lamps on the platform, women coming to our wagon, beefsteak from the train buffet, Caesar's Commentaries! Lavinov, my dreams, and Elizaveta Mikhailovna in a dream. Four trains, one after the other, went past the village in the direction of Feodosiya. After several hours' travel we, too, were already there. It was evening and we were given a room in an empty store, whose bare shelves served as our bed. The store windows were broken, the hollow echo of our conversations resounded in the empty storehouse, and it seemed that it was other people who were speaking and arguing near us, our doubles. In their words there was an ineluctable and sad meaning which we ourselves did not possess; but the echo raised our voices, made our phrases more drawn-out, and as we listened to it we began to understand that something irrevocable had happened. With clarity we heard what we would not have known had there not been an echo. We saw that we would leave; but we understood this only from an immediate perspective, and our imaginations went no further than the sea and the ship. The echo that reached us was new and unfamiliar, as if coming from those countries which we had not yet been to but which we were destined to discover.

When I stood at the side of the steamboat and looked at the burning Feodosiya—there was a fire in the city—I didn't think that I was leaving my country and did not feel it until I remembered Claire. "Claire," I said to myself. And just then I saw her in the fur cloud of her winter coat: Water and fire separated me from my country and from the country of Claire; and Claire disappeared behind the fiery walls.

For a long time afterwards the banks of Russia followed the steamboat: Phosphorescent sand was poured onto the sea, dolphins leapt in the water, the hollow propellers rotated and the sides of the ship squeaked. And below, in the hold, one could hear the sobbing babble of the women and the noise of the grain with which the vessel was loaded. The fire in Feodosiya was getting farther away and looked weaker, the noise of the engines grew more distinct and loud, and then, coming to for the first time I noticed that there was no more Russia, and that we were sailing in a sea surrounded by blue, night water beneath which the backs of dolphins could be glimpsed—and by the sky, which was close to us as never before.

"But Claire is French," I suddenly remembered. "And if this is so, then why was there this perpetual and anxious sorrow about the snow and the green planes and all those many lives which I had lived in a country which has disappeared behind a fiery curtain?" And I began to dream of how I would meet Claire in Paris, where she was born, and to which she would no doubt return. I saw France, the country of Claire, and Paris, and the Place de La Concorde, and before my eyes it looked different from the one which was displayed on postcards, with lanterns and fountains, and naive bronze statues; water continually gushed forth and poured down the figures, shining in dark glitterings—the Place de La Concorde suddenly seemed different. It had always existed inside of me; I had often imagined Claire and myself there, but the echoes and images of my former life did not reach there, as if they ran into an invisible wall of air. Air, perhaps, but just as insurmountable as the fire barrier beyond which there was snow on the ground and where the last nocturnal signals of Russia sounded. Bells rang on the steamboat, and their blows immediately reminded me of the bay in Sevastopol, which was covered with a multitude of ships on which small lights were lit, and at a certain hour on all the ships these blows of the hour sounded, hollow and cracked on one, dull on another, ringing on a third.

The bells rang out above the sea, above the waves slick with oil; the water lapped against the pier and at night the port of Sevastopol reminded me of paintings of distant Japanese harbors asleep above a yellow ocean, so delicate, so inscrutable to my understanding. I saw Japanese harbors and slim girls in shanty houses, their delicate fingers and narrow eyes, and it seemed to me that I imbued them with that special mixture of chastity and shamelessness which compels travellers and adventurers to seek out these yellow shores, this Mongolian magic, delicate and clear as air which has turned into transparent, colored glass. We sailed for a long time in the Black Sea; it was rather cold. I sat wrapped up in an overcoat and thought about the Japanese harbor, about the beaches of Borneo and Sumatri, and the landscape of a smooth, sandy shore where tall palm trees grew did not leave my mind. Much later we were to hear the music of these isles, drawn out and vibrating like the sound of the shivering saw which I still remembered from that time when I was all of three years old; and then, in a flood of instantaneous happiness, I felt the endlessly complex and sweet feeling which reflected in itself the Indian Ocean and the palm trees, and the olive-colored women, and the gleaming tropical sun and the damp thickets of southern plants and disappearing serpentine heads with tiny eyes; the yellow fog rose up over this tropical greenery and magically swirled and then disappeared; and once again the protracted sound of a trembling saw, having flown across thousands and thousands of versts, transported me to Petersburg's frozen water, which, by the divine strength of sound, was once again turned into the distant landscape of the Indian Ocean's isles; and just as in childhood, in Father's stories, the Indian Ocean opened up an unexplored life to me, rising above the hot sand and rushing like the wind above the palms.

We sailed to Constantinople to the sound of the ships' bells; and already while on the boat I began to lead another existence, one in which my attention was turned to the cares of my future meeting with Claire, in France, where I was to go from ancient Stambu. A thousand imagined situations and conversations crowded into my head, each abrubtly ending and superseded by others: But the most lovely thought was that Claire, whom I had left that winter night, Claire whose shadow pushes me into the background and when I think about her everything around me sounds quieter and muffled, that this Claire would belong to me. And once again her unattainable body, still more impossible than ever, appeared before me on the stern of the boat littered with sleeping people, arms and sacks. But the sky clouded over, the stars became invisible; and we were sailing in the sea's twilight to an invisible city; airy precipices gaped behind us, and in the humid quiet of this voyage the bell occasionally rang—and this sound which accompanied us all the way, only the sound of the bell united, in its slow, glassy translucency, the fiery brinks and water which separated me from Russia, with the murmuring and wonderful dream about Claire that was just now coming true.

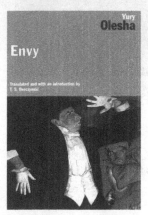
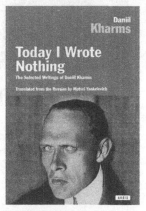